MW00877165

BROKEN TRUST

Written by

Winter Paige

PLAYLIST

I am Light- India Arie

The Lonely- Christina Perri

Little Do You Know- Alex & Sierra

Tell Your Heart to Beat Again- Danny Gokey

Truth Hurts- Lizzo

Sorry Not Sorry- Demi Lovato

Just a Kiss- Lady Antebellum

Bathroom Floor- Maddie & Tae

Perfect- Ed Sheeran

You Are The Reason- Callum Scott

We Were- Keith Urban

Be Your Man- Rhys Lewis

Think of You- Chris Young & Cassadee Pope

Big Girls Don't Cry- Fergie

DEDICATION

This one is for anyone who knows what it feels like to fight to find yourself, to paint on a smile just to look okay to the outside world, or to pretend to be brave just so you can face each day.

To anyone that hides who they are and feels unworthy any time that mask breaks.

You are beautiful. You are worthy. You are the light.

You are worth the wait.

Go sparkle, Princess.

LOVE REMEMBERS

CHAPTER ONE

Eliana

Stumbling, I grip my bathroom vanity, scoffing at the sight of its shining surface. Why even bother cleaning it every other day? Not like I am getting it dirty using any of my products. When I finally look at my reflection, I gasp at the pale girl staring back at me. She's at least 10 pounds lighter, has dark bags under her eyes and a ghostly sick complexion.

She looks nothing like the beautiful woman I was growing into with Joshua... before.

I throw both hands over my mouth to muffle the wail clawing at my chest at the thought of my Charming. I can still feel him in my arms, his blood seeping through my fingers as I begged him not to leave me. Why couldn't I just go with him? I don't want to be here anymore. He was the only one who *really* loved me, and now he's gone. You. Promised. Me. Charming. Why? The pain is unbearable, and even though I'm aware my body isn't quite strong enough to make a run for it yet, I don't have a choice. The pain is shredding me from the inside out; if I don't run, I'll die in here. I am trapped in this prison, faking a drug-induced fog and sneaking in daily walks around my room. No one other than Rachel really comes in here anyways, they won't even miss me. I've been forgotten while they continue their parties as if I'm not lying up here in ruins. They have destroyed me; shattered every piece of my soul. None of them ever really cared at all. I'm nothing more than a game... their pawn. The guys have no idea I have been listening in this whole time. Bargaining and betting. Sling and trade.

I am nothing but a possession to any of them. Then, they sneak in here, one at a time, every few days, to cry over their guilt. Boohoo. You're sorry? *No, I'm sorry.* I'm sorry that I *ever* trusted any of them.

My head is spinning, so I chug another glass of water. It's the only way to flush the remainder of the drugs from my system before I head out. I nearly topple over when I hear the door to my room open, so I throw my hand out, flipping off the light. I sigh in relief when Rachel's singing drifts into the room, knowing that I stand a chance against her small build. Standing just inside my darkened bathroom door, I watch as she moves to my bed and bends to lean over it, looking for me.

"You fucking cunt!" I lunge forward, tackling her, sending both of us to the ground. I straddle her and push my knife to her throat, blinking rapidly to clear my vision.

"It's about fucking time, Lili." She chuckles.

"You fucking drugged me. It's been two months Rachel, and the whole time you have been feeding me pills to keep me fucking quiet!" I seethe.

"I did, but seriously, Lili, do you really think I had a choice? Now, let me the fuck up so we can talk.

How long has it been? I mean, I thought you were pulling out of this at least four weeks ago when I was *accidently* late on your dose, but I could be wrong." Rachel raises a brow.

This bitch.

"If you try anything, I'll fucking cut you. I swear it. Don't fucking push me, Rachel." I rock back on my heels, swaying on my feet. Once she stands, I gesture to the bathroom. "Dump them."

She walks over, opening the bottles and pouring the contents into the toilet and then flushing.

"What about Andr-"

"Fuck him! Do I look like I give a shit about any of that? After everything that happened, you all betrayed me. Every one of you left. I lost him and-" Her gaze softens as she reaches for me, and the dam breaks. "I can still hear him, Rachel. I can feel him. It hurts too much."

"I know. I know, but you are so strong. You can-"

"No, don't do that. It's not about being fucking strong, and you know it. I am completely alone; I don't even know who I am anymore."

A door slams downstairs, and she holds a finger to her lips, motioning to my bedroom door.

Carefully, we make our way over and open it just enough for their voices to drift up to us.

"It's time, Jaxx. I am going to have Rachel start easing her off the meds. You need to get everything in order and be ready. You have the ring?" Daddy slams what sounds like a tumbler to his desk.

"Andrew, she has been catatonic for two months. She hasn't even had time to fucking grieve. She's seventeen. When she comes to, the last thing she will remember is the mother she thought dead stabbing her fiancé. Fuck, Andrew, Joshua bled out in her arms. You are being irrational. Think about it. I cannot propose to her yet, and she will never say yes."

I clutch the locket Joshua gave me for my 16th birthday, still hanging from my neck. He's right; that's all I have, I don't even know where he was buried. I don't remember much of anything that happened those first couple of weeks after he died. After he proposed. My mother better stay fucking dead this time. All this time... all the years she was gone... Regardless of what Daddy did, *she* was the real fucking devil and deserves everything that happened to her. I hate her more than I do them.

She was my *mother*, and from the very beginning, she hated me. Joshua and I were innocent, and yet they targeted us that night. They stole the purest, happiest moment of my entire life and then demolished every part of me. I *hate* them. My only regret, other than not dying with my love, is that her death was too easy. My thoughts are cut short by Costin's arrogant ranting.

"Fuck, Andrew, why him? You know I want her; I'll take care of her! Why not me?" Of course, Costin would throw his hat in the ring. I'm a fucking prize worth billions. However, if any of them gave a shit, I wouldn't be standing here right now.

"You know why, Costin. Don't fucking start with me." Why not him daddy? I mean fuck *all* of you, but why not *him* in particular?

"I think you need to worry more about the fact that the girl is in serious need of a sandwich. Have you seen her lately? How can any of you stand here, talking as if what you are doing to her is okay? She is a fucking shell of the girl she was." Abel stomps into the office, closing the door behind him.

I see red, "Fuck them." If you care so much, Abel, march your big ass up here, and help me!

"Idiots," Rachel breathes out. "You need to get moving."

I march directly into my room, turning to Rachel too quickly, I place a hand on the doorframe to steady myself. "If you're staying, you're keeping your mouth shut. If you tell them anything, I will show you how much like my father I really am. Understood?"

She nods, "And what aren't we telling them?"

"Exactly." I walk into my closet and pull on my tightest black mini then step into my riding boots, placing my Louboutins in an oversized purse for later.

"Huh." Rachel grins. "Big night?"

"I can't do this anymore, I'm done. I'm taking my life back, Rachel. The pain is crushing me, and they-" I gesture to the door. "-can go straight to fucking hell. Let's see how they like being left in the dark."

"Good girl, but what about..." she gestures to my pendant and phone.

"Welll." I drop my phone into the toilet, smiling, knowing that the burner cell in my bag is my real connection to the outside world. "Ooops."

"And the pendant?"

"Oh, I have the perfect place for that to spend the night." I smirk.

"Be safe, Lili." She hugs me tightly. "You will be okay, baby girl."

Sliding open my window, I toss my pumps out, watching my large bag hit the grass with a thud. Slowly, I climb out onto the closest limb. Careful not to fall, I trace the letters we carved the first night Joshua scaled my wall, 'You're worth the risk. J <3 E.'

"I'll be safe, Rachel, but I refuse to die in this room while everyone else goes on living. What about you? What will you tell them?"

"You were gone when I got here, obviously. I told them to bring in a doctor." She smirks. "But you know, Andrew knows everything."

I snort a disgusted laugh. "We'll see."

Once I'm on the ground, I wave back up to her and sway on my feet. I'm not sure how I will get out of here like this, but I pick up my oversized purse and sprint to the garage. No cars. Where the fuck are they? There in the corner is the bike Costin gave me for my 17th birthday. Fuck it. I roll it out of the bay and around the side, out of view of Daddy's office, and then jump on, speeding from the drive, trying my best to keep the bike from swerving. I have a cow to visit and friends to get to. If parties fix the guys' problems, well, it's time for me to give it a try, too.

Pulling onto the dirt road, I ease over the fence and run to the field, calling out as I sprint through the tall grass, pushing aside my nausea.

"Joey Ramone, get your fancy fluffy fanny over here, and love me!" I drop to my knees when I reach him, soaking in this moment, and cry into his fur. He is untainted; he's the good from my childhood, and I need this desperately.

"Can you do me a solid, master J? I need you to hold onto this for me." I secure my bracelet to a lanyard, draping it around his neck, and grin. "Rockin' the bling, you fantastically cute muffin! I gotta roll out before they notice I'm gone, but make sure you move around a lot, 'kay? I'll see you soon. Hearts and stardust, sidekickster!" I blow him a kiss and hop the fence, jump on my bike, and speed off.

Three minutes later, I'm pulling onto the freeway, weaving between cars and pushing myself to dangerous speeds. If I die today, then so be it. At least, I will die free. I tip my head back, sighing. Is this what it feels like to fly, Joshua? A horn startles me, and I narrowly avoid colliding with a pickup. I barely manage to right my bike and pull off on Isa's exit. Slowly making my way through town to her family's modest home, I feel my heart ache with want. I love her house. It's always warm, people laughing or reading, sitting in comfortable worn-in couches. Her mom hugs everyone, dad snores in his chair, and her siblings run around giggling. Her house is made cozy by love. It's a home. She hates it, always complaining about the noise and wanting nicer clothes and shoes. But she's wrong. She has all of the best things here already; she has a family with real love.

I climb off my bike as the girls rush out, and Isa hugs me. "Holy shit, Lili! What the hell? How did you get away?"

"We came to your house every day! I know you said you were fine and you didn't need our help, but Lili, look at you! You're skin and bones, sweetie. It's only been two months! And Joshua..." Nat's lip trembles as they both hold me.

"I don't want to talk about it. I will. I promise. But

It's nice out, and we can talk without listening to them." He hands me two bottles of water and laughs as Isa's screams fill the townhouse.

"Please."

"Through my room – private patio. We each have one." He flips on the lights, and I smile.

"Pretty." I sit carefully on one of the two lounges pushed together and cast in the soft light and open a bottle of water. He's right about the water; I do need it.

"Small deck." He shrugs, flopping down beside me, holding out a fork full of cake. "Open up, beautiful."

Ten minutes, two bottles of water, and three pieces of cake later, Jonah cracks the seal on the vodka. He takes a sip directly from the bottle then hands it over to me.

"Thanks." I nod, swallowing two large gulps.

"That kind of day?" He raises a brow.

"That kind of life." I shrug.

"Yeah, I heard. I'm really sorry. How are you holding up?"

Two more gulps, and I answer, "I'm not."

"Wanna talk about it?"

"I really don't. Opposite, actually. I want to forget." I chance a look his way and continue when I see genuine interest in his gaze. "I just want to be a normal girl for a night."

"I think we can do that." He looks around, suddenly laughing, and smacks my thigh. "We're gonna play a little game the guys and I came up with last week... but with a fun twist. See that box of water balloons in the corner? We're going to finish this bottle while we take those and drop them on the assholes blocking our entrance. Each direct hit earns you one Truth or Dare from the other person." He grins, passing back the bottle, and I drink. Just like that, he's back to the Jonah I danced with at the club, and I couldn't be more grateful.

"Truth or Dare? Jonah, you've just made a huge mistake, the worst truly, because there are two things I never do. One is back down, and two is lose. I'm going to demolish you, rock star." I get to my feet. "Bring the booze!" I call back.

"You have the booze." He laughs stumbling over to me.

"So I do. Shit, someone drank it all." I lift the bottle, shaking it from side to side. That went fast.

Seeing his confused expression, I crack up, releasing my first real laugh in months.

"Holy shit!" The door slides open, and Nat's head pops out. "That *was* you. It was Lili; I told you!" she yells back inside. "I thought you had lost your damn mind." She looks from the tub of balloons and back to us. "Okay, I'm 'a need to know more, just not right now. Keep making her do that." She motions to my smile, winking at Jonah. "Fuck, I missed you, Lili." She closes the door, leaving us alone again.

"Well, that was dramatic." I roll my eyes.

"That's one!" he yells.

"Cheater!"

"Nope! Now, what will it be…" he taps his chin.

"One and two!" I call back, dropping one after another, triggering rounds of curses from below. "Three, ya loser."

"Filth and lies." He looks over at the people below searching us out and quickly ducks back out of sight. "How in the-"

"Watch and learn, peasant." I grin, sliding my small arm through the narrow space in the railing, lining up my shot, and dropping the balloon.

We both erupt in laughter when the balloon

lands with a splash and yelling.

"What did you fill these with?" I sniff, curling my lip. "It's rank."

"Milk. Three days ago." He shrugs, and I double over with laughter.

We talk for hours, always keeping it light and laughing more than I have in ages. He tells me about his tour pranks and the crazy fans and then loses it when I tell him where I left my pendant.

"You're telling me that when they realize you are gone, they will track you but find a fluffy miniature cow instead?"

"Joey Ramone is people; he's a duke for goodness sake. And yes, that's exactly what they will find but with a top hat." I smirk.

"Because he's a duke." Jonah nods, lifting our second bottle to his lips with a grin.

"Obviously." I smile, taking it and drinking.

"That's all the balloons. Who won?" He stands, offering me a hand and pulling me to my feet, but I stumble, falling into his chest.

"A tie?" I blush, looking up at him.

"Nope, I'm clearly the winner tonight." He leans in, brushing his lips to mine, and I release a soft moan at the contact. I've missed feeling this connection with another person. Encouraged by my reaction, he deepens the kiss as I cling to his shirt. Drunk enough to relax and lonely enough to go with it.

He pulls back a hair, breaking the kiss, "Truth or Dare?"

"Truth."

"Can you feel the pull too, or are you just lonely?"

"Both," I answer honestly.

"Me, too." He kisses my jaw then my ear, whispering, "Truth or Dare, beautiful?"

"Dare," I breathe out, closing my eyes.

"Stay with me."

"How long?" I wrap my arms around him, moving in closer.

"We fly out Monday for a month to record. Stay."

"Okay."

"Yeah?"

I nod, and he kisses me again. My legs snake around his waist when he lifts me and carries me to his bed but hesitates.

"We can stop now. Just sleep. Tell me if you aren't ready, beautiful. Either way, I want you here, but I need to know before we-"

I kiss him passionately, pouring everything I have into him. We're normal. We're free. "Don't stop until neither of us can move an inch," I whisper.

Growling, he tosses me to the bed, grabbing the bottom of my dress and ripping it right up the center. "Fucking gorgeous." He takes in my bare chest, breathing deeply through his nose and licking his lips. "Except this." He reaches over, pulling my panties slowly down my legs, and tucks them into his pocket with a grin.

"I might lose this record deal because there is no way I will be done with everything I want to do to you by Monday. Maybe ever."

He pulls his shirt over his head, tossing it to the floor, followed quickly by his pants and boxers. I gasp when he stand straight again.

"Oh, shit." I gape at his rock hard cock. "I don't know if you... I mean... holy fuck... Of course, the rock star had to have a giant fucking cock. You're going to kill me with that thing."

"Oh, we'll fit, beautiful, and I am going to have you begging me to fuck you." He chuckles, stroking his cock and climbing onto the bed. "You're going to do a lot of begging... and moaning." He runs a hand down my body and lowers his mouth to mine, rasping out, "Tonight, you're mine," then kisses me deeply.

"I need to taste you, beautiful." He pulls back and then trails warm kisses down my neck and chest, nipping and licking at both nipples as I squirm beneath him. His hair feathers across my belly as his tongue swirls around my navel and he continues his torturously slow descent. When he finally pushed my legs apart, settling between my thighs, I am on fire, and his first taste nearly sends me over the edge.

"Problem, beautiful?" He smirks.

"No, no problem," I gasp out when his tongue takes another swipe over my clit.

"We have all night. Don't hold back. There will be plenty more. Cum for me." He licks me hungrily, holding tight to both thighs to keep me in place as I explode.

"Oh, Jonah. Oh, God! Oh, please. Oh, yes!"

"That's one." He raises his eyes to meet mine as he slowly begins pushing a finger inside me. "You're so fucking wet for me. I... fuck, you're tight! You aren't a-"

"No." I sit up, looking at him. "I'm not. Once before. No, we aren't talking about it, and yes, I want you. Now." I grab him, pulling him down to the bed.

"Okay," he laughs. "I was only joking about the begging."

"Oh? That's too bad." I grin, climbing on top of him. "Condom?"

He reaches over and passes me one from the nightstand.

"I don't know how to." I gesture down, causing him to laugh.

"Definitely losing that record deal. I am never leaving this bed." He rolls the condom on and looks back at me. "Ready?"

I nod, taking a deep breath as I straddle his hips.

"Give me your hands." He reaches for mine, helping to steady me. "Slowly, okay? No rush."

I lower onto his cock an inch at a time, stilling once he's completely inside. "Holy shit. Holy shit, you're big."

"Fuck," he hisses, "You feel fucking incredible. Don't move." He closes his eyes, breathing deeply, then looks directly into mine. "Ride me, beautiful."

I roll my hips slowly, adjusting to him. When he releases a moan, I ask breathlessly, "Show me what you like, rock star. Teach me." He growls, gripping my hips and moving me up and down his cock, gaining speed with every rise and fall of my body onto his. I feel another orgasm building as I reach up, rubbing both of my nipples. When his thumb finds my clit, I shatter, screaming out his name, and slam down on him.

"Fuck." He flips me to my back, pushing inside me and circling his hips slowly. "That's two." He places my calves on each of his shoulders, running his palms over my thighs. "You good?"

"Oh, God, yes," I hiss when he thrusts into me, pulls out slowly, and pushes back in hard. "Ohhh, yes, please. Harder."

"Oh, I can give it to you harder, beautiful." He grips both thighs, pounding into me, each thrust more forceful, possessive. I feel another orgasm building right as he commands, "Cum for me, beautiful." Thrust. "Cum." Thrust. Thrust. "Now!"

I scream as the orgasm rips through me, burning a path through my body straight to my core.

Leaning forward, he pushes my thighs to my shoulders, and his hips turn punishing. "You are so fucking perfect; I'm going to cum, beautiful. With me, give me one more." He kisses me deeply as another orgasm slams into me.

"Oh, Jonah!" I shout as he growls out his release with a few final jerks of his hips.

"Three and Four." He falls beside me with a grin, pulling my body to his and kissing me softly. I rest my head on his chest and hear it... one. two... one. two. But it's not the same. He's not my Joshua. What have I done?

I need out of here. I roll away, trying to contain my sob until I make it to the bathroom, but Jonah is on his feet in a flash, blocking the door.

"What is it, beautiful? Are you hurt? Talk to me." He searches me with panicked eyes, but I shake my head furiously, knowing if I attempt to speak, I will crumble.

"Eliana." His face softens seeing my heartbreak, and he steps close and pulls me into a hug, "Come here. It's okay, beautiful. Let it out. Tell me."

A sob slips from my lips, and Jonah lifts me as my knees buckle, "It hurts. It's not fair, why him? I want him back."

"I know... I'm so sorry, beautiful." He says, walking us to the bed and wrapping a blanket around my shoulders.

"What have I done, Jonah? Have I completely betrayed him? I do love him. I do! My heart still beats for him," I plead, hand pressed to my heart, begging him to understand, knowing I don't.

"What happened tonight doesn't change the way you feel for him, beautiful. Before-" He swallows. "-you chose him. I remember, and so do you. But, beautiful, he's gone." He brushes away my tears with a sad smile. "Do you really think he would want you to be alone, drowning in sorrow, mourning him for the rest of your life? Or do you think he would be happy hearing your laughter again? From Nat's reaction earlier, I can tell it's not something that happens a lot these days. Big change from the girl full of joy that I danced with at the club."

"He wanted me happy-" I whisper. "-but..."

"No buts, beautiful. He wanted you happy, that's it. Do you honestly think he would put restrictions on your happiness? No. Don't let guilt steal away all of your smiles, Eliana. You need to heal, and locking yourself away isn't the way to do that. You need to let people in. It doesn't have to be me, but I am here if you need me. You aren't alone in this. I kinda like ya, beautiful." He smiles softly.

"Jonah?" He's right. Joshua would hate that I was alone. I desperately need someone in my corner again.

"Yeah?" He gives my hand a gentle squeeze.

"Truth or Dare?"

"Truth." He shoots me an amused smirk.

"Do you really want me to stay? Still?" I watch him closely.

"Absolutely." He places his hand on my cheek, and I lean into him, needing the physical reassurance. "Stay, beautiful. Let me help you find your smiles again." He lays back lifting an arm, and I cuddle in, releasing a deep breath.

"Get some rest, beautiful. You aren't alone anymore. You're going to be okay."

And I do... I still miss Joshua, and my heart still aches for a love that will never again be mine, but I close my eyes, taking this moment for what it is. A reprieve from the anguish, because here with

Jonah, I can pretend to be whole.

Here with him, I'm not broken. Here with him, I'm not alone. Here with Jonah, I'm a normal girl, and that girl is free.

CHAPTER TWO

Costin

Creeping towards Eliana's door, I pause, listening to see if I was followed. I'm getting her out of here. I open her door, shutting it behind me, and creep over to her bed silently.

"I'm here, Princess. It's time for-"

"Oh, holy hell, my prince is finally here! But he's far too late, and look at me without a fucking gown!"

Setting the copy of Sleeping Beauty she was reading to the side, Rachel cackles from the center of Eliana's bed.

"What the fuck, Rachel? Where is she?" I rush to the bathroom, nothing. Closet, empty. "Rachel! Where is she?"

"Gone, shit for brains." She tosses up an M&M from Eliana's nightstand and catches it in her mouth, grinning. "Took me all afternoon to learn how to do that."

Taking a deep breath, I attempt to calm down as I step in close. "Where, Rachel?"

"That I don't know. Seems Aurora finally woke up and rescued herself. Didn't need you all after all... just a forgetful godmother. Anyways, I'm out. Just wanted to see how long it took you all to figure it out." She looks down at her phone, shaking her head. "Sixteen hours just in case you're wondering."

"Can you just fucking answer me?" I bellow as the door flings open, Jaxx and Abel storming in.

"Why are you two yelling in here? You're going to upset her." Jaxx moves over to Eliana's bed. "Where is she?"

"I'm bored with this. Let's skip to the next part."

Rachel flops down on the lounge. "Now that she's realized she doesn't need you all to save her, what will you do?"

"Rachel, I swear if you don't start talking, I will-"

"What, Jaxxson, torture me? Fuck me? Kill me? You can try." She stands, grinning darkly. "But we both know I've lasted this long for a reason. I let her go. I watched that girl lay in that bed for a month, waiting on you all to do the right thing. Thought you had a fucking plan. Pathetic shits left her. One evening, your party ran late, and so did I. Guess those couple of hours gave her just enough clarity. And then, just like her daddy, she waited for the perfect moment to make her move." Rachel shrugs. "I really thought you all broke her, but hearing your conversation yesterday really brought back that fire." She grins.

"Just tell us where she is, Rachel," Abel sighs. "We're garbage. We know. At least, I do."

"Out. She'll be back, but right now, she is making a point, and I suggest you all listen really closely." She steps up to us, lip curled. "You fucked up. You abandoned the only person in this house who ever gave a shit about any of us. And after all these years, she has finally realized that she doesn't need us. *We* need *her*. You can look if you want, but I'll bet fifty blowjobs that you won't find her until she is ready to be found." She walks to the door, looking back over her shoulder. "I love that girl. She deserves a chance, and I can't wait to see what she does with it."

The door closes, and Abel sinks to the lounge. "Fuck."

"What were you doing in here, Costin?" Jaxx studies me.

"Not that it matters now, but I came to get her out of here." I walk to the window, noticing the garage door ajar, shaking my head with a grin, and whisper, "Fucking, Always."

"What?" Abel stands to see.

"Her bike." I nod. "She took the bike. Rachel was right; she's back."

"I've tracked her. Let's go." Jaxx leads us out the door and down to the porch.

"Where?" I ask, climbing on my bike.

"The field. She's with the cow." He shakes his head.

"Figures. We'll follow you, Jaxx," I yell as the

three of us leave in hopes that groveling will be enough to bring the Princess back to us.

Forty-five minutes later, we're stomping through what I hope is mud and realizing that this might have been intentional on her part.

"Son of a bitch! She didn't," Jaxx barks, jogging ahead. Leaning over, he yells, "She did!"

I laugh out when I see what he's holding up. "Is that her pendant? Tell me it was on Joey Ramone!"

"Yeah." He brushes back his hair, looking up to the sky. "Now what? She isn't safe alone."

"Well, seems she wasn't always safe with us, either. I told you all this would happen. None of you listened because you were all too busy fighting over who was right to actually do anything. It's no surprise that she doesn't trust us enough to reach out," Abel says, defeated.

"We were keeping her safe," I argue, knowing it's weak.

"We were letting Andrew keep her compliant and out of his hair, Costin. We all know it," Jaxx bites out, pushing back his hair as we make our way back to the bikes.

"I'm done keeping my mouth shut. Twice, I've

seen things all of you refused to acknowledge, and both times, I stood down, outnumbered. My self-doubt and your bullheadedness left her to fight alone." Abel stops, picking up his helmet.

"She was a mess. She couldn't even sleep without-"

"Without what, Jaxx? Screaming for us? Begging for our help? Sobbing out our names because she trusted us to protect her? To stand by her?" Abel fumes then lowers his head. "A lot of good that did her. We left her to rot instead of helping her. That changes now, and if I have to do it alone, then fine." He pulls away without a second glance, leaving us in a cloud of dust.

"Fuck."

"He's right, Cos. We can make all the excuses we want, but the truth is we left her because none of us was man enough to admit that we could have prevented it. She said she knew I would never let her down, and when she needed me the most, I stood back and watched her fall."

"Look, Jaxx." I pick up my helmet, pulling it on. "We fucked up. I do that. A lot."

"That's the damn truth." He shakes his head.

"Blow me." I flip him off. "Anyways, here's the thing – E forgives me. Every. Single. Time. Not because I deserve it, not because she has to. She does it because that's who she is. She loves hard and fights for the people she loves. So put on your big boy pants, stop with the boohoo bullshit, and let's finish this *with her* just like she asked in that hospital bed. In her heart, she knows we tried to keep her safe. She just needs to be mad first." I grin, climbing onto my bike.

"Last time you just let her be mad, she started dating Laporte." Jaxx grimaces. "Who knows what she's up to now."

Well, that hadn't even crossed my mind. Fuck.

"Let's go," I growl, speeding home. We need to fucking find her.

Eliana

"No!" I yell, scrambling to stand. Where am I? It's so dark.

"Shh, beautiful, you're okay. It was just a dream."

"Jonah?" I feel him reach out, pulling me back to

him.

"Yeah, it's okay. You're safe." He presses his lips to my forehead, rubbing a palm up and down my arm soothingly. "Do you want to talk about it?" he whispers.

"No. No, I just want it to go away." I hurriedly wipe at my eyes, cursing the tears.

"I have them sometimes, too." He shrugs.

"You do?"

"Yeah, some things just stick with you. It gets easier, though, Eliana. Every day, you'll get a bit stronger. You just need to keep moving, surround yourself with people you love, and do things that make you happy. Bring enough joy into your life that the sadness can't reach you."

"You've found that, Jonah? Chased out your shadows?" I whisper.

"Not completely, but I'm getting closer. Come here." He lays us back against the pillows. "Think you can sleep?"

"Maybe if you sing for me." I pout.

"For the girl who thinks I'm dreamy? Anything." He chuckles and begins singing softly.

I wonder how much good it will take to find my

peace. When Monday gets here, I'll have some tough choices to make, but for now...

"Jonah?"

"Hmm?"

"Make love to me again?" "Thought you'd never ask." He grins, rolling me onto my back and carefully pushing inside me. "Keep your eyes on mine, Eliana. I'll help you chase them away. And when we finally sleep, you will be far too happy and exhausted for nightmares." He kisses me and begins slowly rocking into me, over and over, taking his time with me.

When I reach my first orgasm and close my eyes, he softly whispers, "One. Stay with me, beautiful. I'm nowhere near done yet."

So, I do. I keep my eyes on him all through the night, making love and chasing away the bad until the morning light peeks through the curtains and we're completely spent.

"Eleven," he pants as we collapse on the bed and I am pulled into a blissfully dreamless sleep.

CHAPTER THREE

Costin

"Where are you going, Costin?" Abel falls in beside me as I'm heading down the stairs.

"Seriously, man?" I ignore him, moving to the far wall, placing my finger in the seam of the exposed brick, and freeing the hidden door. "I'm getting fucking answers, Abel."

"Where's, Jaxx?"

"I'm realizing that we all seemed to grow balls at the same time. Oh, and that if Andrew kills us for this, I stand a pretty decent chance of getting out alive while he takes down your clumsy asses." He smirks.

"Funny... you in?" I turn, heading down into the basement.

"I'm in. Have either of you seen Andrew's secret guest?" Jaxx latches the wall back into place and follows us down.

Abel shakes his head no, and I could scream. "Are we seriously saying that none of us have been down here? We have just taken his word for it this whole time?"

"He had me on detail nearly 20 hours a day." Abel shrugs. "Didn't think anything of it after what happened. I wanted to be out there."

"Well, I was chasing down leads." Jaxx gives me a pointed look. "How about you, Cos?"

"With Andrew. Playing the role I was supposed to play." I rub my neck, ashamed. "He has been partying a lot, gotten unpredictable, and we have to call for clean up a few times a week. So yeah, it's been... busy."

We're all silent as we make our way to the end of the hall where Andrew keeps his 'long term guests,' and I open the door.

"I fucking shot him!" Jaxx lunges forward, wrapping his hands around the man's throat, squeezing. "You are supposed to be fucking dead, you piece of shit."

"Jaxx! Let the fuck go! Let go! He could have the answers we need to keep her safe!" I yell as Abel pulls him back.

"You perverted piece of shit. How are you even alive?" Jaxx hisses. "Answer me, Puckett! After what you did to her, I will enjoy every second of breaking you. Your death will go on for years."

"I think you should talk dick-bag. He'll do it, and if it will get answers, we won't stop him." I shrug.

"After what I did?" Puckett pants. "I took fucking pictures. I never even touched her. Honestly, didn't even find her attractive until last year. I'm not into kids, and I'm not a fucking rapist. I was just doing what I was told to."

"You didn't touch her?" Abel sneers. "I remember that part quite differently."

"That was the only time, and Vonnie lied to me.

She told me what happened to her and that her daughter was in on it… they were working together to hurt Andrew. She said it was all staged, planned in advance."

"You believed that?" I seethe. "You held her back. That looked fake to you?"

"You didn't know her mother, man. Yeah, I believed it because her mother could have faked those same emotions without trying." Puckett exhales slowly. "I didn't even question it until she raised the blade. It all clicked; when I started to let the girl go, I was hit."

"That's why you hesitated?" Jaxx paces.

"Yeah, man. I watched y'all long enough to know that she had targeted the only innocent ones here. They were spoiled brats but good kids. All of you, on the other hand… you all deserve this as much as I do," Puckett spits.

"Facts man. Why are you telling us this now? You have been here for two months?" Abel leans in.

"Now? I told that asshole everything I know a month ago!"

"Everything? He knows where you hid the photos?" I arch a brow. "And who else you were working with?"

"Okay, almost everything." He smirks. "But fuck that guy. I heard him say I'm a gift for her. You know if she comes down here and gets blood on her hands, it will ruin her, right?"

"You think you know her?" I sneer.

"No, but I knew her mother all my life. Loved her all my life, too. I watched her grow into a girl exactly like yours, marry Xavier Keswick, and live a fucking fairytale. Just to be turned into what you saw the day she stepped into Andrew's world. All over what? Because Andrew's daddy refused to share his last name? Couldn't be the money. Look around you." He shakes his head.

"Keswick? Eliana's birth name was Eliana Keswick? He even took her name from her..." Abel shakes his head.

"Yep. The Keswicks. Don't tell me you haven't even *looked* into where she came from? Who's keeping her safe?" Puckett asks with wide eyes. "Don't tell me it's Andrew?"

"You care? Tell me what we need to know," Jaxx hisses.

"No. Her. I'll tell her. It's her life on that film, her

choice. It's all safe, but I will only show her."

"Wrong answer, asshole." I pull back to hit him when Jaxx places a hand on my shoulder.

"He's right, Costin. However, you can tell us what we are missing. *Who* we are missing."

Shaking his head, Puckett sighs. "I wish I could. I never saw the guy. Heard him once when I called Vonnie. The asshole answered my call and let me hear them fucking. All I can tell you is he's dangerous. Vonnie said he's the coldest man she had ever met, wealthy as fuck, and wanted what Andrew had. Including his daughter."

My blood runs cold. We aren't dealing with a small time idiot staying hidden in the shadows.

"So you're telling me-" Abel starts.

"I'm fucking telling you that your enemy is probably walking among you, with you, and that he has the means and control to make any moves he needs to get what he wants. Andrew may have met his match."

"If I brought you recordings, could you pick out his voice?" Jaxx asks.

"Fuck yes, I could." He nods.

"We need to go; we've been here too long." Abel

stands by the door. "We'll be back."

"Wait! Just in case. Tell her... tell her the truth lies where a false king reigns. Love bug promises, princess wishes, and young love's tortured pains... and... I'm sorry." He hangs his head.

Once we are in the hall, I start, "That was fucking weird."

"That was actually the least weird thing that has happened in months. She'll probably know what he meant." Jaxx unlatches the door, leading us out to the main portion of the basement.

"Now we just need to find-" I spot Richard at the bar watching us. "What the hell are you doing here?"

"Looking for Andrew." Richard shrugs, staring back where we came from, "You?"

"Same." I say when we all sit down on the couch.

"Fuck!" Abel quickly stands and runs up the stairs. "We need to roll."

Following behind, we don't speak until we are sure we're alone.

"What the hell, Abel?" Jaxx huffs.

"I know what she's doing..." Jaxx and I move to either side of him, looking at the screen.

"Oh, for fucks sake, is she cooking? Who the hell is that?!" I yell as Abel turns up the volume.

"Shut up!" Abel growls. Then his eyes soften watching her. "Are they singing? She's amazing. She looks so free." We listen as Isa streams a video of Eliana smiling in the arms of that dick from the club last year. They *are* singing, not even aware they are being recorded. She looks happy, and he looks like a problem. When he kisses her deeply, we all lose it.

"I'll kill him!" I yell.

"Where are they?" Jaxx reaches for the phone, but Abel steps back.

"Use yours dick; we need to split up. Location services are off on Isa's phone, which is good but inconvenient." Abel gets on his bike. "Social media, gossip, twitter. Some weirdo fan will know where to find the band, and that will get us to her. I'm heading out." I look down at my phone, confused as fuck. I don't use that shit.

"Jaxx, man, what are we looking for?"

"3J, the band. Says here that's Jonah." He curls his lip, pointing at the screen.

"Does it say where they are?"

"No, just that they fly out tomorrow to record in

LA and that they are somewhere around here until then."

"You think she would go to LA?" I panic.

"I think she's pissed and drinking. So yeah, she might end up in LA. Hit the streets. Find out something, and stay in touch. I'm going to find Andrew before he hears about this on his own."

Heading into town, I both want to find her and I hope that Abel gets to her first because I will gut anyone that touches her.

Andrew

"What do you mean she's gone? How?" I bellow. If someone took her, I will burn this entire state to ashes.

"Andrew." Richard turns the laptop in my direction with a smirk. "Looks like she ran off to party."

"Yeah, seems our girl is pissed at us and found a very dramatic way of showing it." Jaxx leans against my desk, rolling his eyes.

"And the medication?" I raise a brow.

"Andrew, really? She is your daughter, and she grew up with all of us. Does it really surprise you that she found a way out?" Jaxx snorts.

Good fucking point, but I don't like it.

"Get her back here now! I won't be disobeyed. I want everyone out looking, and when she is found, bring her to me. It's time I have a serious chat with my daughter."

"Andrew, remember she is 17." Jaxx stands and walks to the door. "I'll bring her home, but if you push too hard, she will just push back. Drugging her was unfair. She's not weak; she's Eliana Jameson. We are the ones who forgot that, not her. Don't push. Apologize. Trust me." Jaxx walks out. He makes sense.

"Apologize?" Richard snorts. "What a little bitch. So, you admit you're wrong and what... let her call the shots now?"

"Get out, Richard. I have to find my daughter. The day I answer to anyone is the day I'm in the fucking ground." He's right. Admitting I was wrong isn't an option. I did what I thought best for all of us. Let her have her fit. She will be back.

LOVE REMEMBERS

CHAPTER FOUR

Eliana

"You are a shit cook, E. Never again. Someone call for takeout. She burnt the pizza bites." Jeremy fans the smoke as Isa giggles, holding up her phone.

"Okay, Nat, your turn." Isa hands her phone off to Nat, joining us in the kitchen with another bottle of rum.

"You two are too cute," Nat yells over the music

as we pass the bottle around, and Jonah leans over, kissing the tip of my nose.

"Dance with me." He takes my hand, spinning me in his arms when Just a Kiss by Lady Antebellum comes on.

"Only if you'll sing for me." I grin.

"Only if you'll sing it *with* me. I mean, unless you're scared." He raises a brow.

"You're on, rock star." I grin at his shocked expression when I start in on the first line, singing and dancing through the entire song.

"Well, you sure are full of surprises." Jeremy laughs beside Nat when the song ends. "You bewitch Jonah, *and* you can sing? Hell, bring her to LA with us."

Jonah smiles, kissing me. "You're something else, ya know that? Not many girls would have sung while all of our followers watched."

"Wait, what now?" Fucking hell.

He points to Isa, laughing, and wraps me in his arms. "Embarrassed now?"

"Embarrassed? No, never. However, seems my hiding is over," I whisper.

"Come on." He takes my hand, leading me to the

me back and kisses me deeply.

"Don't forget me, beautiful."

"Impossible." I smile, touching a finger to his dimple. "Goodbye, Jonah." I walk to the door, pausing when he calls out.

"Abel, if anything happens to her, I'm coming for you."

"Anything happens to her, you won't have to." Abel places a hand on my shoulder. "Thank you for taking care of her."

"I'm pretty sure I was the winner there." He smiles at me, and we turn to head home.

Climbing onto the back of Abel's bike, I can feel Jonah watching from the patio, so I yell up.

"Make LA your bitch, Jonah." I blow him a kiss, and he grins, catching it. "And sing for me."

Thirty minutes later, Abel and I are pulling off the road by the clearing.

"Why are we here, Abel?"

"Come on. We're doing what I should have done for you two months ago."

"I can't," I whisper, my whole body trembling and pulling away. "Abel, I can't do this, please."

"You can, and you will. You want to move on?

You want to heal? You have to start here. We are going back into the pit, but you have to face this first." He takes my hand. "You don't have to do it alone. I messed up before, but let me help you now."

I nod, walking the path in silence. Letting go of his hand, I step over the fallen tree with a sob. A few more steps, and I'm standing in the spot where Joshua proposed to me, where we lost our virginities together, and where he died. My knees buckle as a scream rips from my very soul, but instead of hitting the ground, I'm in Abel's arms.

"Let it all out, Darlin'." He holds me until I am all out of tears and my sobs have gone quiet.

"I have so much hate inside me, Abel."

"Use it." He lifts me to my feet. "You have to leave the tears here though, Darlin', and cut out the partying. You had your fun, but I need you clear headed for this. You know the world we live in, and those things will make you vulnerable. You want your justice, Eliana?"

"More than anything." I suck in a breath, standing taller.

"Then fucking take it. This is it. I'm with you." He kneels in front of me, taking my hand. "I will never fail you again. I have found my voice. Now the question is will you find your sword?"

"Abel, I never lost my sword." I help him stand. "I just didn't realize I still needed it. My eyes are open; let's head home."

LOVE REMEMBERS

CHAPTER FIVE

Costin

"He has her." Jaxx stands from his bike, walking to me. "Kick off your lights."

"Say where?" I turn off my bike, leaving us in the dark.

I want to, but it's probably best I not know where to find Jonah. I saw the video. Hell, Jaxx said there were four hundred-thousand views within the first three hours and thousands of comments asking about Jonah's new love. Just what we needed, more eyes on her.

"Safe and close," Jaxx huffs, turning toward the sound of Abel's bike as it slows to a stop.

"The hell, big guy? Why are we out here? You know that Joey Ramone is in for the night, and I'm not wearing that pendant. Plus, bugs, man..."

"We need to talk." Jaxx steps into Abel's headlight, and she immediately looks pissed. I have never seen her look at him with so much disgust.

"Great, come on out, Costin. I know you have to be here, too." She jumps off the bike and marches our direction.

"Munchkin, let us explain." Jaxx reaches for her hand, but she quickly yanks it away, causing him to flinch.

"Oh, no. Nope, this wasn't a little mistake, Jaxxson. You all left me. I trusted you, *all* of you, and you failed me completely. I would never have done that to any of you. Ever," she shouts.

She's right. She would have killed herself fighting for any one of us.

"Princess, we were wrong. We just didn't know

how to help. Your pain was-" She raises a hand, halting me.

"Mine, Costin. My pain. For me to deal with however I needed to in order to make it out the other side. You all took that away from me." She stands taller, shoulders back, eyes blazing. "I'm taking it all back. Now. I'll fight whoever I need to in order to set this right. Does that fight include the two of you?" She looks from me to Jaxx.

"No, Munchkin, never. I'm so sorry. We just wanted you safe. We were wrong." He pulls her into his chest. "Forgive us, please."

"You, Jaxx. Out of everyone, I never thought you would abandon me." She hesitantly wraps her arms around him. "You were always in my corner."

"I never left. I just made a bad call. I'm here, whatever you need. I'll do anything." He steps back, looking her over, brow furrowed, "Are you okay? What are you wearing?"

"I'm fine, and that's none of your business." She shoots Abel a pointed look. "I took a break."

"A break?" I arch a brow, causing her to turn her anger on me. Shit.

"Yes, a break, Costin. I did what you all do every

chance you get. I had fun, and I'm not sorry. He... it gave me the time I needed to clear my head. I lost everything-" Her voice breaks, but she closes her eyes, breathing deeply. When she opens them again, her resolve, her strength is practically radiating from them. "I lost everything. Everyone. My whole life, I was a pawn in someone else's game and didn't suspect a thing. Never once did the people I loved and trusted the most tell me the truth. So, now is your chance to start fixing this guys. Be honest. What are you hiding from me?" She looks us each in the eyes, one by one.

"Munchkin..." Jaxx hesitates.

"Take me to Isa's house to get my bike, Abel. We're done here." She stomps across the gravel road.

"Puckett is alive, and your father has him in the subbasement!" I shout desperately.

"He what?" She freezes mid-step as Jaxx and Abel curse.

"That's what you lead with?" Jaxx hisses and then speaks to her. "Let's back it up a bit, okay? What do you remember about... that night?" he ends softly.

"Everything, Jaxx. I remember every second.

Every sound, touch, emotion, pain, taste... I remember everything. Sometimes, I wish I didn't, but I do. And every time I close my eyes, I live it all over again." Her chin trembles, and I cross the distance between us in two swift steps, taking her in my arms and kissing her head.

"I fucked up, Princess. I never should have walked away that day," I whisper, thinking she won't grasp my full meaning.

"I don't blame you for not wanting me, Cos. *I* don't even want me." She breathes out, breaking my heart as she steps back. "What else? I know there's more."

"There is, but we don't know much. We're pretty certain you are still being watched; however, the threat is bigger, wealthier, and smarter than we originally thought. Leads keep turning up dead, and the ones that do live are useless. That's why we wanted you safe; someone is obviously toying with us," Jaxx explains, rubbing his neck.

"Uh-huh, great job, guys, really. So what you are saying is you fucked me over for nothing?" she huffs. "How about we try a new approach, just for fun, all right?"

"Which is?" Abel reaches across, poking her side.

"I help you. Tell me what you're looking for, and I help find it. Hell, I may already know something. No one has ever watched what they say around me, always treating me like I am clueless. You have *all* underestimated me, and that is finally going to work in our favor." She bites down on her thumbnail, thinking.

"And how will that work, Munchkin?"

"We fall in line." She shrugs. "This disappearance was nothing more than a tantrum. I'll go back to being the spoiled brat, giving him what he wants with my usual flair and ridiculous spending habits. Once things settle, I will find out what we're missing."

"You know what he expects from you, right?" Jaxx asks cautiously.

"Oh, things changed while I was being drugged?" She rolls her eyes. "No? Then, he wants my inheritance and us married. So we give him one hell of a show. Once he's convinced and we have what we need, we make our move. Whatever we decide. Together. After the past few days, I know exactly what I want. I am done being pulled around. Now, what about Puckett?"

While Jaxx explains everything we learned from Puckett, I watch her closely. She's strong, but she's shaken to the core. I'm worried she'll crack; it's a lot for one person to deal with, and she's much too calm.

"What's that supposed to mean? Love bug promises and princess wishes? What king? Guys, my tiaras and love bugs are in daddy's safe. I outgrew those years ago." I snort a laugh. She's full of shit. "Blow me, Cos. They got too small. What I have now are *hair pins,* not tiaras. Educate yourself." She sticks out her tongue at me.

"Watch that tongue, Princess." We go silent when our phones chime.

"It's Andrew. We need to go. So, it's agreed? We all play along?" Jaxx slides his phone back into his pocket.

"It's the only way to end this." She nods. "Anything else?"

"Whose clothes are you wearing?!" I have to know. I bet they are his. Don't be his. She needs to change.

"Of all the questions." Abel shakes his head.

She smiles down at the t-shirt and sweats double knotted at the waist and rolled at the ankles, running a hand over them fondly. "Someone who helped me chase away the shadows and find a bit of calm."

Jaxx and I grumble while Abel smirks. "Didn't seem calm to me, Darlin'. Looked like a tornado hit you."

"Abel!" she shrieks, and then incredibly, she laughs. "It *was* calm... in between."

"I might puke." I cough.

"Fantastic," Jaxx growls. "Now I have another stop to make."

"Listen to me, both of you!" she snarls, "If either of you go near him, I will *never* forgive you. Ever. Understand? He is an amazing man, and he was there for me when neither of you were. I won't let another life suffer because I touched it. I'm not a child anymore, so stop!"

"Okay, Munchkin. Just, was he... good to you? Respectful?" Jaxx huffs, pushing back his hair.

"The best. He saved me." She looks to Abel.

"I hate it, but I have to admit he impressed me." Abel nods.

"Cos?" she questions.

"Him, Princess?" I force an amused grin. "You're choices are questionable, but okay. Besides, he's headed to LA." I laugh as she runs at me.

"You already knew!" Launching herself onto my back, she wraps her arms around my neck. "He's dreamy... and way better than basement whore," she adds, whispering, "and don't forget I chose *you* once upon a time... might want to watch your insults." Hopping down, she places a quick kiss on my cheek then runs to join Jaxx. "Guess I'm yours now."

I flinch. "Ready for this, E?"

"Hell yes! It's time we take control of their games!" She snaps her helmet, wrapping her small arms around Jaxx. He places a hand on her arm, rubbing it for a moment before returning it to the handlebar and heading in the direction of home.

As I ride behind them, my soul screams. I *still* choose you, Princess. Always. Nevertheless, I push it away and focus. One thing at a time.

LOVE REMEMBERS

CHAPTER SIX

Andrew

Pulling up to our house, I don't even wait for the driver to get my door before I am storming up the stairs to my daughter's room. I have had all of my men out searching for her for over twelve hours. If she thinks for one second that I will let this go, she is mistaken. I stop outside her door when I hear Jaxxson's raised voice.

"... Unacceptable, Eliana. I don't care what your reasoning is. It was careless, and as your soon-to-be husband, I will not tolerate your disobedience. Your father and I agreed it was for the best. You could have been hurt, love. Don't let it happen again, understood?" Jaxxson asserts, surprising me. Good.

"Yes, Jaxxson. No more drugs, please." She wines. There's the daughter I know.

"No more drugs. We have a wedding to plan and very little time."

"Shopping?" she squeals.

"Shopping." He chuckles.

I have heard what I needed to, so I knock once and walk in.

"You're home, Poppet." I narrow my gaze on her as she pouts.

"She is, Andrew. Seems our girl had decided to throw a bit of a tantrum." Jaxx stands, placing a hand on the back of her neck, and uses his thumb to tilt her head, locking gazes with her. "However, that won't be happening again. Will it, baby?"

"No, Jaxx." She turns to me. "I'm sorry daddy. I didn't like the meds, and I missed my friends."

I cross the room, sitting beside her. "Something

to tell me?"

"What do you mean, Daddy?" she smiles looking down at her feet.

"Perhaps you would prefer to sing it to me?" Jaxx growls as her eyes go wide. "Poppet, never again. You painted a bigger target on your back. You are not to leave this house again without clearance from Jaxxson or myself."

"Daddy..."

"Eliana," Jaxx says firmly, and she nods.

"All right, Daddy." I raise a brow at Jaxx, and he laughs.

"Tell him the rest, baby." He motions to her.

"Jaxx asked me to marry him."

"And?" I raise a questioning brow.

"Look at my big ring, Daddy!" she holds out her hand. "So shiny. Oh! I need the black card. We're going shopping."

"Beautiful, Poppet. Tomorrow. Get some rest. It's late. Jaxxson, I would like to speak to you in the hall."

"Goodnight, Daddy. I love you." She stands, heading to the bathroom with her clothes. "Jaxx?"

"I'll be back." He follows me into the hall.

"Care to fill me in?" I hiss.

"We found her and brought her home just like you asked. She was still pissed, so I figured I might as well put it all out there at once." He shrugs, grinning. "By the way, I told her you didn't set a budget for the wedding."

"No wonder she agreed." I chuckle. "Whatever it takes, Jaxxson. You staying with her tonight?"

"Yes, I'm done for today and want to make sure she is settled before heading back out. I sent Abel and Cos on to bed; we have been going for over forty-eight hours and need to rest." He turns to leave, but I speak, stopping him.

"Jaxxson, don't fuck this up. Keep her happy and in line. If *you* can't do it..." he knows what's on the line.

"I can handle her, Andrew. You saw her submit in there. Nothing to worry about." He walks into her room, shutting the door behind him.

Not sure how he did it, but he did. Everything is falling back into place, I just need to tie up some lose strings.

Eliana

Once the guys step into the hall, I take a quick shower, letting the water beat away the tension in my shoulders, and release a deep breath. It was over the top, but I think it worked. Daddy needs to believe that I will obey Jaxx when I would normally buck anyone else. It's not a hard push since I have always trusted him without question.

I step out of the shower, drying off. I study the ring Jaxx placed on my finger moments before Abel informed us of Daddy's arrival. It really is beautiful, a flawless diamond set in an antique band. He did well.

I wipe the condensation from the mirror above the sink and reach for my toothbrush, freezing when I notice Joshua's still cradled next to mine. My heart aches, and I suddenly feel sick. Running to the toilet, I hit my knees right as my stomach revolts and empties its contents into the bowl. I flush, turning to sit once I'm sure it's passed, and wrap my fingers tightly around the locket and engagement ring hanging from the chain around my neck.

"I'm so sorry, Charming. I'm not replacing you.

Please come back to me," I beg then cover my mouth with both hands, smothering a sob. I can do this. I can fake it, make *all* of them believe I'm fine.

"Munchkin?" I scramble to stand but stumble, falling back to my knees when I hear Jaxx enter the bathroom. "Careful, baby. Dizzy? Want something to eat before bed?" He lifts me into his arms, carrying me to the bed, and lays me down gently.

"No, just tired I think; been a long day. Are you staying?"

"Of course. I won't leave unless there is work to do and never without telling you." He takes off his shirt and climbs into bed, wearing the pajama pants I bought him last Christmas after walking in on him in nothing but his boxer briefs, and then pulls me to him.

"Did he buy it? Played it a bit alpha, didn't you, *baby*?" I poke him in the side, stressing the word baby, teasingly attempting to lighten my mood.

He laughs, flipping me on my back and tickling me. "As a matter of fact, he did, and I didn't *play* alpha, *baby*. Andrew knows us, and if we are going to sell this, we have to be as real as we can. The less we lie, the less chance we have of fucking up. Got it?"

"And *baby*?" I laugh. Holy shit, that's kinda hot, but he's still *Jaxx.*

"Felt right. Not sure Munchkin works if we are supposed to be engaged." He shrugs and brushes my hair back, kissing my forehead. "We should probably get some rest. Hard to tell what tomorrow will bring."

"Goodnight, Jaxx." He pulls me to him again, and I cuddle back in with a sigh.

"Sweet dreams, Eliana." He quiets before softly asking, "You do forgive me, don't you?"

"Of course I do, Jaxx. You're still my person. You just made a bad call," I hug him tightly. Holding up my hand, I ask, "What about you? This ring should be on the finger of a woman you are actually in love with, not mine."

"That ring is right where it belongs; we're going to be okay, Eliana."

"I love you, Jaxx."

"I love you, too. Rest, baby."

Costin

I wake to a pounding, and my door swings open, slamming into the wall.

"Get up. Andrew wants all of us in the basement now." Abel tosses me the pants from my chair.

"It's still dark. What the hell happened?" I pull on my jeans, grab my keys and wallet, and step into my boots.

"Something about the Laport house. I don't know exactly, but from the way he's acting, it's bad." Abel glances across the hall to E's door. "Have you seen Jaxx? His room is empty."

"We can peek in, but don't wake her."

"Costin... we promised."

"To stop hiding things from her; I know, but she just got back, and we have no idea what's going on. Let her sleep, and we will fill her in later if this turns into anything. Why wake her just to sit here and worry?"

I tie my shoes and stand, stretching. We cross to her door and creep over to her bed, watching them sleep. Lucky bastard is wrapped around her like he's afraid someone will steal her away in the night. Can't say I blame him.

"Jaxx," I whisper, pinching him hard under his

arm.

His eyes snap open while he pulls his Glock from the nightstand, leveling it on my chest in the blink of an eye.

"Fuck, man. On edge?" Abel laughs as Jaxx lowers the weapon, tucking it away.

"With her safety, yes." He tugs the blanket up around her shoulders, "Why are you two here?"

"Andrew needs us. Immediately." I motion to the door.

She stirs, and he runs his hand up and down her back soothingly, "It's okay, baby. Go back to sleep."

What. The. Fuck?

He slides out of the bed carefully, looking back at her sleeping form. "I told her I wouldn't leave without letting her know."

"So write her a note. We have to head down before Andrew comes looking for us." I toss him a notebook and pen from his desk.

"Okay. I need to get her a new phone." He scribbles out a quick note and sets the notebook on his pillow. Then, we follow him into the hallway.

"Baby?" I mock, "Really?"

"Don't fucking start with me, Costin. She might

be back, but she's not *back*. I'm doing everything I can, but sounding like a fucking pervert by calling her Munchkin while we are engaged didn't seem like the best move."

"I hate this," I seethe.

"Well, get over it. We have bigger issues." Abel walks ahead of us. "Douglass Laporte's home was broken into a few hours ago. We don't know why, but-"

"About fucking time! We're heading out now!" Andrew storms towards us, out the door, and onto his bike. "It's connected. I know it is."

"He's riding?" Jaxx asks, eyes wide.

"He's doing a lot of things these days, *brother*." I shoulder past them and out the door, climbing onto my own bike and pulling out of the circle after Andrew. The faster we find answers, the faster I can get my girl back, and I want her back now.

CHAPTER SEVEN

Eliana

Rolling over, I notice the cold bed beside me and sigh. Day one, and I am alone... again. Oh look, a note. Goodie.

Baby, had to help Andrew with something. Not sure what yet, but I promise I will be back as soon as I can. Sorry I didn't wake you, but you were sleeping so well, and I didn't want to ruin it. I'll have a phone for you later today.

I Love you, Jaxx

Well, isn't that just fantastic. Guess I may as well get up. I dress comfy, forgoing shoes, and head down to the kitchen for a bottle of water.

"Oh, Richard, hey." I start when I see him in the kitchen.

"You're back." He smiles. He really is a handsome man. He and daddy always gather attention from the women at my school. It used to bother me, but not so much now.

"Enjoyed your show, sweet girl." He tickles my ribs, and I blush.

"Saw that, did ya?"

"Sure did. Care to dance?" he laughs holding out a hand, I place my much smaller hand in his, and he quickly spins me into his body.

"There's no music, Richard." I laugh as he sways us from side to side.

"Oh, no? From what I remember, you are pretty fantastic at making your own." Blushing again, I duck my face into his chest. I always envied Bethany for having such a kind father. Quick with the compliments and warm, this is what I wanted with my dad. What I got was a fucking show.

My lip trembles, and I sniff at the thought. Richard slows the dance and tips my face up to his with a pointer finger under my chin.

"What is it, sweet girl?"

"I'm sorry." I shake my head. "I'm okay, just-never mind." I step back and grab a water from the fridge.

"Eliana, you know you can talk to me, right? You can *trust* me."

"It's not that. It's just..." I sigh. "Richard, do you ever feel like you are missing something? Like something big is happening right in front of you, but you are the only one who doesn't see it?" I ask, watching his reaction closely for deceit.

"Sweet girl." He hugs me tightly. "Sometimes, people are just trying to protect you." I start to speak, but he shakes his head. "I have kept quiet for a while now, but with Bethany missing, I am really worried about you. I don't think you have been properly looked after lately. I stayed behind when I noticed everyone we trust leaving. I don't think you should be alone here."

"Everyone is gone?" Now that he mentions it, the

house is unusually quiet.

"Yes, and you just proved my point. You had no idea you were alone. What if someone were to come in here and..." He shivers. "Anyways, sweet girl, I think you should come stay with me at the beach house for a while, make sure you are protected until all of this passes. I can help them keep you safe."

"Thank you for the offer, Richard." I hesitate but smile. The guys would freak if I went anywhere, even with Richard. "I'm okay, really. I left because I wanted to. I was angry, not scared." I squeeze his hand, hoping it reassures him.

"Ah, before I forget," he pulls a small box from his pocket, handing it to me. Oh, I love Richard presents!

"Richard." I gasp as he places the small box in my hand.

"Wait just a second, sweet girl. It's not what you think."

"It's not?"

"No, sit down." He guides me to a bar stool. Sitting down on the one beside me, he turns me to face him, placing my knees between his, and my stomach drops. This can't be good.

"You're scaring me, Richard."

"I know," he huffs. "I've waited too long, I fear, but with what your father did to you after the... accident. I didn't have much of a choice. I knew you would want this, and I'm hoping it doesn't set you back. I had to pull a lot of strings to get you some of his ashes and-"

"His ashes?" I rip the lid off of the box and pick up the small heart shaped pendent with angel wings wrapped around its edges. Releasing a sob, I read the inscription. "'She used to be my Angel, but now I'm hers.' Oh God." I clutch it to my chest, falling forward and landing in Richard's arms, releasing a wail only comparable to those ripped from me *that* night.

"Oh, Sweet Girl, I'm sorry. I'm so sorry. Maybe I was wrong? I fought them on it. I really thought you would want it, and I knew-" He reaches for the tiny urn, and I pull back.

"No, Richard, no. It's okay. I'm okay. I just didn't expect it, and the inscription, it's perfect... it just hurts, ya know? Thank you so much for doing this for me. For fighting for me." I sniffle, attempting to compose myself.

"They said you needed to forget. I just didn't think that was fair. When my wife passed, I... never mind. I just thought this would help. He's with you, Eliana. I know you can feel that, but now you have a physical part of him too. I'm so sorry you hurt, Sweet Girl." He wipes the tears from my cheeks, holding my face in his hands.

"Yeah, I do feel him." I glance up the stairs, thinking about last night. "I miss him so much, Richard. I just wish I could go back." I sniff.

"I know, but you are so young. You will be okay. Things will work out; just wait and see. Now, how about I help you with that?" He gestures to the pendant. "I assume you want to add it to the necklace with your ring?"

"Yes, please," I stand, turning my back to him, lifting my hair from my neck, and allowing him to slide the small urn onto the chain to join the other important pieces.

"There, perfect." he adjusts the charms and places them back against my chest. "I need to be going, but before I go, I want you to think about the answers you are looking for. Eliana, you can't un-know unpleasant things, and sometimes those things can alter your entire world. Consider the cost before you go looking, okay?" He looks meaningfully into my eyes.

I nod because I truly do understand.

"Okay, if you decide it's worth the risk, I think you already know where you should start." He glances in the direction of the basement door and back to me. "Sometimes you have to dig a little bit deeper to find what you're looking for. An extra layer if you know what I mean."

"I think I do, Richard. Thank you."

"Let me know if you need me, okay? I know your dad can get busy, but I'm only a phone call away. I'm here for you, sweet girl."

"Thank you for being honest with me, Richard. I don't get much of that." I hug him tightly.

"Thank you for trusting me, Eliana. See you soon." He rubs my back then turns and leaves the house.

Looks like I'm checking the basement then.

LOVE REMEMBERS

CHAPTER EIGHT

Costin

Once we arrive at the Laporte place, Douglass meets us on the porch.

"Took you all long enough," Douglass huffs out, clearly out of breath.

Opening and closing the door a few times, Abel speaks up, "Someone kicked this in?"

"That's what I told Andrew. Can we focus on

something we don't already know?" Douglass rolls his eyes and turns to Andrew. "They were in Joshua's room. I have no idea what they could have taken, but his desk has been emptied, and someone was in his computer. I haven't been in there since... well, you know."

"Yes, let's take a look. Jaxx, you're with us. Costin, you and Abel look around down here." Andrew heads up the stairs, shooting back a look that I know well: *What's Douglass hiding?*

"Cos, someone kicked in this door? What's wrong with this story?" He steps back, allowing me a clear view of the frame.

"What the fuck? There's no damage to the jamb. The deadbolt was locked?" We both look back at the door. "No fucking way. Look at the print on the door, clean. It should at least be smeared a bit, and only one kick opened it? This door is solid."

"*If* someone came in this house, it wasn't this way, man." Abel nods up the stairs. "He just sat his fat ass here and waited for us? Something isn't right."

"Yeah, why target Laporte anyways? After what happened with Eli-" My blood runs cold, and both of our eyes go wide. "Who is with her? We're all here!"

"Jaxx! Home!" Abel shouts on my heels, running back down the walk to the bikes. We speed back home, hoping we're wrong and knowing that whatever this was, it was probably meant to get her alone.

Eliana

Deeper, huh? I walk to the brick wall at the back of the main room in the basement that I saw Daddy disappear through years ago. I never made it down there because Abel stopped me, but like Richard pointed out... no one's here to stop me now. Shrugging, I feel around the exposed brick for-there it is. I compress the button and gasp when the door slides open after hearing the clicking of the lock disengaging.

Well, well... can't get much deeper than this. I giggle. I've gotten hella sloothy. Too bad the guys are too alpha macho dumb to appreciate it. Richard is the only one who has looked deep enough to see how strong I really am. I'm going to figure this out and shove it in their grumpy faces.

At the bottom of the stairs, I enter a short hallway with two doors on each side and one at the far end. I check each room as I pass. They look like cells, but they are all empty. This must be where Daddy is keeping Puckett. Costin did say the subbasement. I hesitate at the last door, wondering if he's tied up.

Reaching out, I slowly turn the knob, hoping to catch him off guard so I can slam it shut again if he isn't restrained. The room is dark, and I'm immediately overwhelmed by a revolting smell. I breathe in heaving when the thick, slightly sweet air hits my tongue, but I search for the switch. Feeling around on the wall, I nearly gag again when my fingers slide across the tacky switch and quickly flip it up, freezing when the scene in front of me is revealed by the overhead bulb.

"No!" I scramble to leave the room, but my foot slides beneath me, and I land with a squish in the puddle of blood. Puckett's dull eyes are frozen open in fear, his throat slashed, and blood is still dripping from the tabletop his body is slumped over. I try to stand, but my bare feet slide in the slightly warm blood. I reach up, trying to pull myself from the carnage, but my hand lands on something small and soft. I pull in a trembling breath and squeeze my eyes closed in an attempt to calm myself. Opening my eyes, I look to the table, seeing Puckett's tongue right where my hand was. Screaming, I pull myself to my knees and crawl out the door, sliding painfully across the hard floor.

Once in the hall, I kick the door closed and pull myself up by the handle then bolt towards the stairs, my slick feet slipping only once in my retreat. When I hit the basement level, I turn, sliding the wall back into place, putting another barrier in-between us, and run again, not stopping until I have locked myself in my bedroom.

Ripping my bloody clothing from my body, I leave a trail of gore from my door to the bathroom. I crank on the hot water and step under the scalding stream, scrubbing my body raw as my knees give out. Richard was right; I can't un-know, and I will never be able to unsee... what kind of monster is capable of that kind of torture?

Costin

I burst into her room with Jaxx and Abel right on my heels.

"Blood, it's- *Eliana!*" I shout, running for her bathroom where I hear the running water.

"Baby? Where are you?" Jaxx shouts.

We all freeze when we find her bright pink naked body rocking on the floor under the shower. I reach for her, shouting back.

"Kill the water; it's scalding! Get me a towel!" I move to touch her, but she jerks away.

"Princess, are you hurt? What happened?"

"Did you all kill him?" she whispers.

"Kill who, baby?" Jaxx walks around, draping a towel around her, and I lift her from the floor, carrying her into her room. Sitting on her bed, I rock her soothingly, earning a nasty look from Jaxx. Yeah, fuck you, too.

"Puckett... he's... they cut out his tongue," she stutters.

We all go white.

"His what?" Abel whispers.

"Did you all kill him?!" she shrieks. "So much

blood! You aren't those monsters, are you? Please, don't be monsters. You're good. You're mine." She shakes, looking at each of us with wild eyes. "I know you. I know all of you. It's not you; that's not you."

"No, Princess. We didn't do anything like that. We were at... out working. We didn't hurt anyone today. I swear it." I hold her close, looking at Abel and Jaxx. "You all want to go find out what's going on?"

"There's so much blood, too much." She shakes her head, looking into my eyes. "I thought I could- I was wrong."

"It's okay, baby. We will take care of it. Costin, you have her?"

"Of course I do. Go. Call Andrew. He needs to get back here."

"I'll be back, baby. Do you need anything?"

"Just hurry back, Jaxx. He was right; it's not safe here. Not safe."

Fuck, I think she's in shock.

"Okay, baby." He leans over and kisses her temple as I continue to hold her. "Rest, okay? You *are* safe. We will always put you first." Jaxx turns to leave, but Abel kneels beside the bed.

"Your sword, Princess. Sometimes, battle gets bloody, but remember what you are here for and *who* he was. Whatever you saw down there, it has no power over you. You've beaten worse."

Her eyes lift to his in understanding, and she touches his cheek, whispering, "Thank you."

He stands with a nod and places a kiss on her cheek before following Jaxx from the room. Whatever he meant with that weird shit, it seems to have gotten through to her.

"Costin?" She whimpers.

"Yes, Princess?" I rub up and down her bare back soothingly, feeling her trembling slow, but not stop.

"Don't let go yet, okay? Stay?" She clings to my shirt, breathing me in. Like I would ever willingly leave her.

"Always." I squeeze her tightly.

"Costin?" As she pulls back slightly, her hair falls, curtaining her face, but I can still see her wide eyes peeking up at me, lashes batting in mock innocence.

"Yes, Princess?" I know that look. She is going to ask me for something... and she knows she will get it. Anything. Always.

"I just realized I'm pretty close to naked." She

blushes, smiling mischievously. Rotten girl is playing with fire.

"Yes, Princess. You are," I rasp out.

"Is that a bad thing?" she wiggles, grinding her ass into my already hard cock.

"Depends on your definition of bad, Princess." Please, let it be the same as mine. If there is a God, let it be dirty.

"Brave Knight?"

"Yes, Princess." I chuckle huskily. Hot. Mess. She is still a hot mess, and she *still* has me wrapped around her finger, especially when playing this angle.

"Make me forget. Give me something good." She turns, straddling my lap, and kisses me. I growl when she lets her towel drop open slightly, exposing her from the waist down. "I have heard all about what you can do. Make *me* feel good this time?"

"Are you sure, Princess?"

"With you? Always," she whispers in my ear, biting gently.

I flip her to her back and lay my body on top of hers, deepening the kiss. When she reaches for my belt, I still her hand.

"I am not fucking you right now, Princess. I will not rush with you, and they will be back soon." She whimpers. "But there is plenty of time to make you feel good." I grin, kissing her.

I push her thighs apart, making sure her towel still covers her upper half, and lower myself to the floor, yanking her ass to the edge of the bed. "Get ready because you are going to cum hard and fast, Princess." I bury my face in her pussy, breathing her in deeply with a moan, and devour her. Pulling out my cock, I pump into my hand as I eat her, imagining it's my dick that's making her squirm instead of my tongue. I lick her relentlessly, focusing on her clit, and right when she begins to beg, I push in two fingers, curling into her g-spot, and she explodes.

"Costin!" she screams my name in a way I have only dreamt of, and I blow my load all over my hand.

Sitting up, she is breathing heavily and looks down at my cum covered hand and cock.

"I would have done that for you, ya know?" she purrs. Well, I really like this new side of her. She gets down on the floor beside me and leans over, her bare ass on display. She licks the cum from my fingers and moves over, cleaning my cock the same way.

"Oh, fuck," I moan out, right as the door swings open, and a very pissed off Jaxx walks in. "Damn it."

"Jaxx, I'm-" She quickly stands, eyes wide.

"It's okay, baby. Go get dressed. We're going shopping." Jaxx motions to the bathroom, and she nods, scurrying away. Once the door is closed, he spins on me.

"What the fuck? I was gone for twenty minutes, and you had her on her knees, licking your cock?!"

"Man, that was all her." I grin, tucking myself away.

"The fuck it was. She isn't-"

"Oh, she is." I nod, knowing I shouldn't but unable to stop smiling. My Princess is a dirty girl. "She asked me to give her something good to make her forget what happened."

"You couldn't just get her some cake?" Jaxx hisses.

"I had pie." I chuckle, and he socks me in the jaw. "Fuck! Look, I'm sorry. I couldn't turn her down. I have waited my entire life to be with her, Jaxx, and she wanted me. I can't be sorry."

"Well, Costin, it can't happen again. What if I had been Andrew? She is engaged to *me*. If he had seen that... it would ruin everything."

I sober at the thought. "Yeah, man. I just didn't-"

"Think. You didn't think. You have to start. Puckett *was* killed, brutally. Someone cut out his tongue. She saw some fucked up shit, and her prints are all over it. We have called in a crew, but I want her out of the house for it. She tracked blood all the way to the main floor."

"Fuck, that much?"

"The worst I have seen since Bethany-" he hisses, "-and you need to prepare for a possible fallout with her. You both acted impulsively."

"But Jonah," I growl.

"Doesn't live with her... he isn't her family. He was a fling. *Yo*u mean more. Whether you realize it or not, you just added a complicated layer to your relationship right after Joshua. Tread carefully, brother." He walks to the bathroom, knocking lightly and going in, closing the door behind him.

Well, fuck...

Eliana

Standing at the sink, I stare at my reflection through my tears. What have I done?

"I'm so sorry, Joshua. I don't know what I was thinking. I was just so-" I sob, wrapping my hand around the tiny urn. "I'm garbage. I did those things with you literally laying against my heart."

I turn on the water, filling my hands and splashing my face in an attempt to hide my torment, then begin brushing my teeth. One of them will surely come to check on me any minute. I look down at my necklace, pieces of time, of love. Pieces that I have now betrayed. I didn't feel this guilt with Jonah. I knew Joshua wouldn't like it, but he would understand my need to *feel*. With Costin, he would never understand. There is no justifying it; I may as well have spit on everything we ever had. I've betrayed the man I love with the only man he was ever threatened by. The one man I swore I would never be with because I love Joshua that much. My thoughts are interrupted by a knock, and Jaxx immediately walks in.

"Gee, thanks, Jaxx. What if I had been naked?"

"What if?" his eyes travel the length of my body before giving me a pointed look, and I realize that my towel is gaping open...again.

"Fuck!" I grab my towel, pulling it closed. "Sorry."

"It's okay, baby." He clears his throat. "Are you all right? That was..."

"I'm a horrible person, Jaxx." My lip trembles.

"No," he rushes over, holding me as I cry. "You aren't a horrible person, E. You are just struggling to deal with all of this any way you can. Cut yourself some slack, baby. You have been through so much."

"Is Costin mad at me?"

"Mad?" He laughs. "No. No, he's not mad. Seems you two had a pretty good time?"

"Jaxx," I sigh, "it was wrong. I just... I needed someone to help me block it out. With Jonah-" His whole body stiffens. "Ya know what? Never mind. It was wrong. It won't happen again."

Nodding, he says, "Well, for now, I think that's a good idea. Remember, Eliana, the less we lie about, the less we have to hide, and the better we can play this. Never say never, just not right now."

"No, Jaxx, never. It can't happen, not after Joshua. I can't." He opens his mouth to speak, and I cut him off. "I can't handle the guilt, Jaxx. So please, just drop it."

"Okay. Ready to go shopping?" he squeals.

"Were you attempting to sound like me, fiancée? Because that was shit." I laugh.

"Oh, I'm your fiancée now?"

Frowning, I step into him. "Jaxx, I really am sorry. Yes, fiancée. That is if you still want me?"

"I'm kidding, E. Of course I still want you." He tugs my towel closed again. "Now get dress; we're dress shopping."

"Dress?"

"Yep, wedding dresses," he says with wide eyes.

"Oh, my God." I laugh. "Is it sad that I am ridiculously excited for this?"

"No, it's not sad at all, fiancée." He kisses me gently, surprising me. "Think you can sell this?"

"I... yeah. Yeah, I think I can." I smile, kissing him back sweetly. "It should be weird, but it's not. Right?"

"Nope." He smiles, shrugging.

"It's because you're my person, Jaxx. My very best friend. Now get out so I can dress." I laugh.

"I think your modesty went out the window

thirty minutes ago." He chuckles, walking out the door as I throw my towel at him. Damn, I think he's right.

LOVE REMEMBERS

CHAPTER NINE

Costin

"Fucking wedding dresses… we're stuck here cleaning up, and they are off shopping for wedding dresses?" I kick the bloody chair across the room.

"Yep. Can you not make a bigger mess?" Abel walks over, picking up the chair, and smashes it against the wall, sending wooden pieces all over the floor. "At least make your messes productive. Help me gather this shit and toss it in the bin to be burned."

"Whatever, man, have you seen Andrew?"

"Yep."

"And?"

"Basement... high as fuck. Gonna need a crew up there before the night is out. He's not happy." Abel stomps to the bin, dumping the wood.

"Fucking fantastic. What girls are with him? Will they be missed?" Fucked question, I know, but the last thing we need is some kindergarten teacher showing up here, thinking she is going to explore light BDSM and then never making it home.

"Richard had them screened." he shakes his head. "It's fucked."

"At least, E is out 'til later tonight. Wedding dress or not, she doesn't need to be here," I shoot back.

"About that..."

"About what, Abel?"

"He's not bringing her back here tonight. They are staying in the penthouse downtown. Jaxx thinks it's best she not come back to all this tonight, and it helps to sell the engagement."

"The fuck? He didn't even tell me."

"*I* didn't want to tell you," he scoffs.

"We are supposed to be in this together!" I fume. "Why am I being left out of the fucking loop?"

"Why, Costin? Why?" He stomps over to me. "Because you can't see clearly when she is involved. How many times have I had to tell you this? How many times do you have to be told to take a fucking step back? I heard about what happened when we left her with you. Are you trying to get yourself killed? Are you that stubborn that you can't let someone else take care of her?"

"No, Abel, I'm not *that* stubborn, I love her *that* much. Every time I step back, she gets hurt. I want to wrap her up, take her away from all of this shit, and never fucking look back."

Deflating, Abel places a hand on my shoulder. "I know you love her, man. You know that isn't an option right now though, right? She can't... she won't walk away. She needs this closure, and Andrew will never let her go. Not to mention we don't even know who the other enemy is yet. You really want to spend the rest of your lives looking over your shoulders?"

"She really needs this?"

"She does, Costin. We can help her, or we can watch her burn. I am done just watching," he huffs. "What about you?"

I nod.

"So play the part, Costin." He walks to the door, calling out to the cleaners. Turning back, he adds, "Worry about the rest later. You have waited this long for her. What's another few months?"

An eternity when I have to watch her with someone else.

"Uh, Costin? Seems we have a situation. We need to roll." Abel pokes his head back into the room.

"What? She okay?"

"Ummm, well. Depends," he says with a grimace.

"Depends? On what?" I look over his shoulder at his cell. "Fuck."

"Yeah, seems the media found E at the bridal shop, and they are clearly hashtag team Jonah. Let's roll." Abel storms from the room, shaking his head. "She couldn't have picked some nobody to play around with?"

"Princess never does anything small, Abel." Never.

Eliana

Spinning slowly in a beautiful off-the-shoulder, lace, mermaid, Vera Wang gown, I smile when I hear Jaxx's quick intake of breath.

"You quite literally took my breath away, baby."

"You like it?"

"You look stunning, Eliana." He walks up to me, holding out a hand to help me down from the pedestal.

"It is lovely, isn't it?" I reach for his hand but gasp when he swoops me up in his arms, spinning me.

"Yes, you are." He laughs, "We'll- what the fuck?!"

We turn and are suddenly bombarded with cameras and yelling.

"Eliana, who is this?" one man yells.

"Eliana, where is Jonah? Are you eloping? When is the wedding?" a women shouts from the back.

"You bitch, he's mine!" A girl shouts from the door.

"Fucking hell." Jaxx curses, pulling me into the back room.

"I've called the police; they're pulling up out front now. The photographers were sticking to the sidewalk, but when they realized you two had come in *here,* they pushed through. Sorry, I didn't want to ruin your day." The clerk approaches us, handing me my clothes. "You can change in my office. I'm afraid the whole world will have seen you in your dress soon, though."

"Fantastic." I walk into the office and lock the door, quickly changing back into my Gucci dress and Louboutin heels, and head back out to Jaxx.

"Costin and Abel are here, baby. They had the car brought around back and are going to help get you out of here. Head down, and walk fast, okay? I would carry you, but-" He shrugs.

"Yeah, no. I can walk just fine." I force a smile. "It's not my first rodeo."

"Let's do this then. Ma'am, have the dress delivered to the address I gave you. We have other plans for the evening." Jaxx hands her a tip, and we quickly make our way to the employee entrance. When we step out, Abel and Costin are immediately at my side.

"We've gotcha, Princess." Costin places a coat over my head, and the guys surround me, walking quickly to the waiting car. I flinch with each flash but make it in one piece.

"Well, that sucked." I pout, sitting in the limo, looking at three smirking men. "What?"

"You are the one who decided on the rock star." Abel laughs.

"You are all garbage humans. Truly." I laugh, flipping them off as we pull away, and then hold out my hand. "Give me your phone, Abel."

"Better idea." Jaxx hands over a phone. "Yours. Try not to put this one in a toilet."

"Oh! Thank you." I kiss his cheek. "Is it the same number? " I look down at my suddenly ringing phone.

"Hello?"

"Hey beautiful, I just heard the great news! We're getting married?"

"Hey, Jonah, yeah." I laugh. "We were just accosted by not only paparazzi but also jilted fans. Fun times. Where are the milk balloons when I need them?"

"So, what's the real story, beautiful?" he says with a serious tone. "I have asked that you be left alone and that the nature of our relationship is our private business. Any outlet that refuses to honor that request will be blacklisted on our end, but *I* want to know. Why are you in a bridal shop?"

"Long story, rock star." I look to the guys, noting the irritation on Costin and Jaxx's faces, although Abel seems to be enjoying this far too much. Whispering into the phone, I continue, "We can talk when you get back. Go be famous already. Plus, I have yet to hear my song. Beauty, grace, excellent aim, all that." I laugh.

"Fucking amazing tits, wizard at sucking dick." he chuckles.

"'Bye, Jonah!" Costin yells, causing Jonah to laugh.

"Okay, beautiful, call me when you have time… and privacy."

"Okay, 'bye, Jonah. Stay safe."

"You too, love." He disconnects.

"That was…"

"Yeah, we know." Jaxx crosses his arms.

Andrew

"About fucking time you all got back!" I bark when

Costin and Abel walk into the basement.

"Not like we had a choice there, boss. She needed help." Abel rubs his neck, "We cleared the penthouse and set up additional security. She will be safe there until this shit passes."

"What's all that?" Costin nods to the table.

"Coke." I laugh, leaning forward, snorting two quick lines, then toss the small metal straw to him, "Here. Then I'll show you what I found while you all were dealing with Poppet's fucking mess."

"Puckett?" Abel coughs, wiping his nose with his sleeve.

"Nothing. No one saw anything. Richard was with Poppet, probably the reason he didn't notice someone but quite possibly what saved her from being hurt as well." I slam a fist to the table. "Who the fuck is this guy?"

"So what's in the folder?" Costin tosses the straw back to the table, sitting back.

"This is what I found in Joshua's room when Douglass went downstairs to see what you all were shouting about. The hard drive was gone from the computer and desk was empty, but this folder-" I spread the contents across the glass top. "-was taped to the underside of his desk. Impossible to see with the drawer in, but when I pulled it out, I felt a frayed piece of tape. It has been removed multiple times before, but the contents were quite interesting."

Costin picks up a photo and quickly puts it back down, turning away. "They are fucking kids! Did you know Douglass Laporte was into this shit? He was around E!"

"Douglass never touched her. It's just these two, look." I shuffle them around. "Same two, for *years.* They are close to your age now, it seems, Costin."

"We don't deal in kids, Andrew! How did he get them? Keep them hidden? Did you know?" Abel says, slamming the folder, but his gaze locks on the young woman in a photo.

"I know we don't deal in children, Abel. And as much as I hate to admit it, no, I didn't know about this. Seems Joshua did, though. Remember the file I sent him away for? *These* kids were in the photos with him. Especially *her.*" I point at the girl in the picture. "I thought... *fuck.* I thought he was fucking her."

"This girl... Andrew do we know this girl? She's

so- familiar?" Abel says, not taking his eyes off the young beauty. I can't blame him. She is gorgeous. Honey brown eyes, dark brown hair, with an hourglass figure most women *and* men would kill for.

"I can't say for sure, Abel. Costin?"

"Once, I think? Maybe a dancer? I remember no one was allowed to fuck her. Douglass was adamant about that." Costin paces. "What does any of this mean, though, Andrew? Joshua knew?"

"It looks that way, but I think he was trying to help them. Look at the letter." I slide an envelope across the table.

"Angel?" Costin questions. "No way she knew."

"Just fucking read it." I roll my eyes.

"'*Don't open the envelope of photos... I'm sorry I didn't tell you... I wanted to help them... Give this to Jaxx... trust no one else... Abel and Costin are too close to do this alone... I love you, and I'm so sorry.*' Holy shit, Andrew." Costin flops against the back of the couch. "We're too close? What is that supposed to mean?"

"That is what we are going to find out. I want Jaxx back here. Don't say a word to Poppet. Joshua was right to keep this from her. Seems they may have come from the same group that had her." I puff out. I fucking hate pedophiles. Always did, but finding my Poppet in that basement really ignited a blazing hatred in me for them. It's not something I tolerate, and it will need to be corrected. Just not until my daughter is safe and settled into her new life.

"You think he had something to do with what happened with E?" Abel asks, still clutching the photo in his hand.

"No, at least, not directly. He lost his son and his chance to attach himself to our family... our money. No, he didn't do that, but Joshua's knowledge? That could have." I lean forward, pulling in another three lines from the table. "There is only one way to find out..."

"A party?" Costin asks.

"Set it up. Mixer..." I laugh. "Every VIP has to bring a minimum of two guests. Show and tell night. No exceptions. Watch for them, boys."

LOVE REMEMBERS

CHAPTER TEN

Costin

It's been fifteen days since Jaxx decided it would be best for them to hide out in the penthouse while we figure this out. Fourteen days since Andrew went on a bender and demanded Jaxx leave her here and come home. Thirteen days since I've seen her, nine since she has answered one of my calls. Seven days since Jonah made his final public statement on their him. He is dead because of me." She lifts the bottle from the ground, chugging the remainder of its contents before I can take it from her. "I don't deserve to be happy, Cos. And I certainly don't deserve to be loved."

"And me?" I beg, devastated now knowing the true depth of her torment.

"I ruin everything and everyone I touch, brave knight." She leans back against the wall, closing her eyes. "Haven't you heard? I'm poison."

She goes silent, seconds later succumbing to the alcohol. I lift her from the cold concrete, carrying her unconscious body to the bed, sitting and cradling her to my chest, and sob into her hair. My strong, brave Princess is far more broken than any of us realized, and we have failed to see it *again.*

I make the call to Jaxx, explaining a little of what I found here and refusing to bring her home like this. The media might have disbursed, but one photo of her unconscious, and new stories will circulate. She has been through enough. We both have. So, I am taking a night to hold the girl that I love and can't have in my arms. She might be out cold, but I hope she can feel the love and safety I am blanketing her in and find a little peace tonight. I will free her from this hurt even if it kills me.

Eliana

I wake warm, held tightly in someone's arms. Turning, I expect to see Jaxx and gasp when I am met with a set of deep brown eyes.

"Morning, Princess. How do you feel?"

I sit up quickly, "Holy shit, we didn't...?" I lift the covers, sighing when I notice I am semi-dressed.

"No, I'll try not to take offence to your relief. Am I so disgusting?" He chuckles when I smack him in the face with a pillow.

"Um, no. I suppose not, but I do prefer to remember the people I sleep with." I laugh. Grabbing my head to stop the spinning, I ask, "When did you get here?"

"Yeah, you were pretty trashed last night, Princess-" he pulls me back to his chest and hands me a bottle of water and aspirin. "-near the bottom of the bottle. Care to explain?"

"Nope, I was just bored. Nothing to explain." I

stand, heading to the shower, and grab the open bottle from the side table. Lifting it up, I take two long swallows and set it back down. "Hair of the dog, yeah?"

"Whoa, Princess. It's ten a.m." He stands, walking to me.

"Just taking the edge off, Cos. Chill. Care to join me?" I grin, motioning towards the shower, and his eyes go round.

"I-" he stutters, but the door opens, and Jaxx strolls in, followed by Abel.

"Rise and shine, baby. Time to head home." Jaxx steps over, hugging me, and I plaster on a smile.

"Andrew wants to see you, Darlin'. Breakfast?" Abel lifts two bags and a carafe of coffee, waggling his brows.

"Perfect. I'm going to shower and dress. Can you guys call down for my things to be packed up and delivered to the house?" I walk into the bathroom, shutting the door behind me. I really hope drunk me didn't run her loud ass mouth last night. That whiney bitch needs to learn how to shut the fuck up.

Costin

"She smells like a fucking brewery," Jaxx hisses as soon as the door closes behind her.

"That's because I'm pretty sure she has spent the past week drinking nonstop." I pace.

"How many fucking bottles did she order?" Abel walks around, gathering the empty containers and setting them on the counter, one by one. "There are ten here so far. Anyone see any food?"

We all look around. "Half a pizza." Jaxx holds up a box.

"That's it? We have to do better, guys. She's self-destructing right under our noses," I huff, falling into a chair and pulling at my hair. "Last night was..."

"Was what, Costin?" Eliana walks out of the bathroom in nothing but a bra and panties while running a brush through her hair.

"Princess, you were wasted."

"So? I was bored." She shrugs. "Jaxx, sweetie, can you pass me the sequined pink Armani?"

He walks it over, helping her step into it and zipping up the back.

"Stunning." He runs a hand down her arm, and I resist the urge to rip it from his body. "What is the occasion?"

"Going to see Daddy, and you know I always like to sparkle." She laughs. "Manolo Blahnik sandals? No, silver please."

Abel hands them over, and she slides them onto her feet and then walks straight to the door with her handbag.

"They are bringing my things, correct? Daddy needs to see how well I listened. I stayed put the whole time... good thing I had the internet and his black card." She winks, walking out, and we quickly follow.

I don't know which Eliana this is, but I don't trust it. Something is brewing, and all I know is that I will damn well be there to catch her when she falls this time.

LOVE REMEMBERS

CHAPTER ELEVEN

Eliana

If I have learned anything, it's that men get straight up dumb when you're naked... or close to naked. I have also learned that they talk too damn much about the wrong shit. Like who cares how much I drank? What matters is that they left me... *again.*

Over. It.

It's time to figure out what Puckett meant. Riddle

me this, Eliana... ugh, total shit show. Can't believe I left these guys at the wheel. Daddy wants me home, coolio. Looks like I am going to be inserting myself into his nasty ass old man parties to get my answers. I hope they are ready for me to shake shit up because I am tired of waiting. At this rate, someone will sweep in and kill me before they figure out anything. Lord forbid they step out of their den of sin long enough to focus on me for once.

Walking into the house, Jaxx places a hand on my back, attempting to guide me to my room. Not this time, *baby.*

"Or not. Watch this, guys." I march straight to the basement before they even have a chance to stop me.

Passing the bar, I call over my shoulder, "Hey, Richard! Daddy this way?" When he moves to stand, I laugh. "Don't get up. I'll find him." He is just having a drink, thank God. That could have been hella awkward.

I nearly puke when I find Daddy, though. Dear God, I never think... add this to the 'can't unsee' list. Oh well, go with it I suppose.

"Hey, Daddy. Don't mind me. I'll wait. I lean over

with a shrug and brush roughly fifteen lines of coke from the glass tabletop with his coat, hop up, sitting and crossing my legs, and then pull out a file, pretending to work on a nail. Okay, part of me is doing it to seem unfazed... the other, more nauseated part of me is avoiding the fact that my dad is getting his dick sucked literally two feet in front of me. Gag. No, mega gag.

"What the fuck?" Daddy yells, and I smile inwardly cause I sure as shit won't be looking up.

Andrew

"Eliana, get up." Jaxx places a hand firmly around her arm, and I notice a slight tremble in his hand. He's scared, good. Time to show them both what happens when he can't control her.

"Jaxx, baby." She turns, batting her lashes, probably realizing for the first time today that she is in over her fucking head.

"Yeah, Jaxx, baby," I mock, "She marched down here. Show her what that entails."

"Andrew..." Costin begins.

"Both of you." I laugh. May as well give him a little action. I have been buying him girls that look like Eliana for years. This time, I can save my money and give him the real thing.

"Andrew, you aren't thinking clearly. She-" Abel stutters. I want to laugh. Fear will get them back in line. Push them just enough.

"No. I am thinking just fine. I am sick as fuck of my daughter throwing these tantrums. You, Eliana, are a Jameson! You have been handed a life sheltered from all of this, but you keep forcing your way back down here. Not even two weeks ago, we had to clean your bloody handprints off most of the house. A murder that *only* traced back to you." I narrow my gaze at her. I know she didn't do it, but there was nothing left for us to gather because she practically rolled through the scene. "So, daughter, step up or get back in line. You can lead like a fucking Jameson, or go back to being my sweet little Poppet. You decide." I see the resolution in her eyes, and I would be proud if I wasn't so fucking pissed.

"You heard him," she sings sweetly, stepping into Costin and pressing her body to his, then reaches behind her and pulls Jaxx to her back. "You too, fiancée."

This fucking hardheaded girl is definitely my daughter.

Costin leans in, kissing her as Jaxx lowers the strap of her dress, biting her shoulder. When both of their hands ease under her dress, causing her to moan, I snap.

"Take it somewhere private. I won't have her put on display. Look around you, boys." I announce, noticing for the first time the crowd that has gathered at the sight of my daughter. "Pick a room, and show her what she's pushed to be a part of."

Nodding, Costin throws her over his shoulder and heads up the stairs.

"If we're finding a bed, it's not one down here," Jaxx replies, watching them go.

"Jaxxson," I call him back as Costin disappears up the stairs with her. "This is your last warning. Get her and keep her under control. She has no idea what she is pushing for. She could have walked into a much different situation today. She is my daughter, my only daughter. Take better fucking care of her."

"I will." He nods, turning to follow, no doubt

"So, before you go diving over anymore balconies, remember that you are pulling all of us over with you," Costin says, taking my hands and helping me up, wiping the stray tears from my face.

"I'm sorry, guys. I'm just... I don't know. Tired of fighting, I guess. Will it ever end, or are we playing this game forever? The wedding is in less than two weeks." I look down at my feet and sigh when their phones sound, no doubt pulling them away from me again.

"It's Andrew. We have to head out, baby."

"Yeah." I flop back to the bed. "I'm going to call the girls. I just really don't want to be alone tonight, okay?"

"They have to come here, Darlin'. You can't go out. It's all hands on deck. Please, don't make us worry tonight. I love you, but my heart can't handle much more this week. Let us focus on solving this puzzle, and then you can have all the girls' nights you want." Abel chuckles, hugging me tightly.

"I miss our girls' nights, Abel." I laugh with him.

"Soon, Darlin', soon. We'll be out shaking our sexy asses in no time." He swats my behind and heads out the door.

"I'm here, Princess, Always," Costin promises, walking out the door. If only it were that simple.

"I love you, baby." Jaxx kisses me sweetly. "Please, please listen to me. We can't push this. You know what the alternative could be. Help me; don't fight me. We are in this together." He spins me in a circle and tickles my ribs. "I want to dance, too, damn it."

"Together." I smile up at him, brushing a kiss to his jaw. "I'm sorry, Jaxx. I will behave. Please, just... check in?"

"I will. Be safe, and be smart, baby. Keep the girls in here. It's not the best idea, but it's the best we've got for now. We'll get through this." He walks to the door, giving me a sad smile. "I love you."

"I love you too, Jaxx." I watch him leave, the soft clicking of the closing door feeling more like the slamming of my prison cell.

LOVE REMEMBERS

CHAPTER TWELVE

Eliana

"Come on, Lili. Let's go out. I'm bored." Isa whines from my bed, holding out our second bottle of whisky.

"Look, I told you all I can't go out tonight. After everything that happened with the paparazzi from my time with Jonah, I can't go out without protection, and Daddy gave my detail the night off.

No security, no leaving the house." I half-lie, flopping down beside her.

"Speaking of Jonah-" Nat sits down beside us, holding out her phone. "-say hi, ladies."

I grin at the screen, seeing an exhausted looking 3J smiling back at us.

"Hiii!" we yell together.

Jonah holds up a finger, winking and walking away from his bandmates. Weird. Then, my phone rings.

"Hi, Jonah," I laugh taking in his mischievous grin. "How is rock stardom treating you?"

"Exhausting." He chuckles. "Enough about me. Am I getting an insider look into the life of Eliana Jameson? Holy shit, that's a lot of pink! Is that a *castle* above your bed?"

"Oh, now come on, Jonah. A castle above a princess's bed is about as common as a groupie *in* a rock star's bed." I laugh, walking into my closet and shutting the door to keep out the snoops... also known as my girlfriends.

"Not this rock star. I don't see the appeal." He shrugs.

"Whatever," I tease. "I remember a certain singer

pulling me up on stage and asking for a night with me before-"

"Before." He laughs. "Anyways, show me around your room, I want to see everything. Where are you right now?"

"This, my dear friend, is my closet."

"Your closet? There are photos on the walls!" He rolls with laughter. "It's bigger than the tour bus!"

"Well, to be fair, nearly everything is bigger than the living quarters of a tour bus, rock star." I roll my eyes.

"No, beautiful, I mean the whole bus." He chuckles then squints. "Now, show me the pictures on the wall behind you. Are those of you? You look so young."

"Yeah, I was nine in that photo. It was my first birthday here. That's me, Jaxx, and Costin." I smile at the memory of them gifting me the princess room I had secretly been wishing for.

"You all were adorable. And that one is Christmas? Who is the girl?"

"That's me and Bethany. I think we were ten? Anyways, we got matching bracelets that year. Cos and Jaxx set up a tree in my old room, so we celebrated in there that night, away from the adults." I'm hit with the memory of a promise that nearly brings me to tears.

'Slowly she opens the box and cries again when she picks up the delicate rose gold bracelet. "The love bug."

"Uh-huh, and look at the clasp."

Turning over the bracelet, she reads the inscription on the added charm.

"Love remembers. Your sister, E." She throws her arms around me and hugs me tight.

"Sister?" she whispers.

"Yep, forever and ever, Bethy. I love you." I hug her back. "I'm sorry about your daddy. My daddy forgets sometimes, too. I'll never forget you, though."

"I'll never forget you either, Lili. Merry Christmas."'

"And that one?" Jonah breaks through my fog.

"Yeah, that's not long after Costin was shot."

"He was shot?!"

"Yeah, on my birthday, no less. Our house was targeted and - wait." Something itches at the back of my mind...

"Wait what, beautiful? What's going on?" Jonah

asks.

"The truth lies within the false king's reign. Love bug promises, princess wishes, and young love's tortured pain. How did I frikin' miss that?" I jump up, running from the room and down the hall to the library at full speed. Pulling back the carpet in the corner, I feel my stomach turn when I see the old blood stain from *that* night. I carefully remove the loose board beneath and then pick up the small box hiding below.

"What is it, Eliana? Talk to me," Jonah begs from the discarded phone at my side.

"Lili, what the hell are you doing? What is that?" Nat walks in after me.

"I don't know, Nat." I look down at the treasure chest Bethany and I decorated in love bugs and tiaras in my hands, its contents dating from a time when we were still sisters. A time long forgotten. "Jonah, I am going to need to call you back. I'm okay, Natalie is here."

"Let me talk to Nat, okay, beautiful?" I hand the phone to her and lift the lid carefully, squeezing my eyes closed, afraid of what I will find inside.

"Okay, I won't leave her. Promise, Jonah. Yeah.

Okay. 'Bye." Nat hangs up and hands me my phone. "What is it, Lili? Oh, my God!"

"What?!" My eyes snap open.

"I totally forgot you all were like besties." Nat laughs. "Look how weird looking she was! OMG, you have always been adorable, though." She lifts a photo from the box, revealing a purple zip drive and a small bracelet that clatters to the ground. I quickly snatch up the drive and slide it into my pocket when she leans over to pick up the small bracelet.

"'Love remembers. Your sister, E.' Wow, Lili, not gonna lie. Feeling a bit salty right now." She laughs, obviously trying to lighten the mood. "We are going back to your room and totally ordering custom bestie bling that will put these to shame! Is that it?"

"Yep," I turn over the box, shrugging, and laugh. "Guess I got excited over nothing. Let's go back to my room. Did Isa crash?"

"You know it. Girl can't handle her booze." Nat pulls my bedroom door shut behind us. Our eyes go wide when we hear laughter coming from the phone sitting on Isa's chest. She is passed out cold and draped over my lounge, snoring. Loudly.

"Hey, guys." I laugh picking up her phone.

"Shameful, truly, you should treat my girl better!"

"Doing okay there, beautiful?" Jonah asks quickly, walking up behind Jared and Jeremy when he hears my voice.

"Yep, got excited over nothing." I smile, shrugging.

"Just an old bracelet and pic." Nat holds them up.

"Aww!" Jared and Jeremy sing.

"Asses." I chuckle. "Anyways, false alarm."

"Uh-huh..." Jonah seems unconvinced.

"Goodnight, guys." Nat and I blow kisses and wave, hanging up.

When Nat finally crashes while texting Jared, my phone chimes with a message.

Jonah: *I know there is something else going on.*

Guilt.

Jonah: *Call me if you need me. Call me if you don't need me. Call me if you are lonely, scared, tired, confused... just call me. I need to know you are okay. You can trust me. Please.*

I reply quickly.

Me: *I'm fine, rock star. Probably nothing.*

I walk to my closet with my phone, laptop, and the zip drive, and then pull the door closed behind me. Sitting in the floor, I lay my phone down and plug the drive into the USB. I am shaking when the digital folder finally pops up on my screen.

A video titled 'watch first' sits at the top of a list of hundreds of image files. Clicking the video, I gasp when I see Bethany's face pop up on the screen.

'Okay, so I don't even know why I am doing this. It's my just in case, I guess.' She shrugs, looking behind her and listening to someone yelling outside of her closed bedroom door. *'Hi, Eliana. If you're watching this, then that means I was wrong. Which probably means you will never watch this.'* She snorts. *'I'm hoping that by hiding the zip with the photo and bracelet, you will know that these images are genuine. Only the two of us know about this spot... well, three now, I guess, since I told Puckett as a backup, so they should be safe. He's not that bad. Dumb as a box of rocks and tangled up in some shit, but aren't we all. Anyways, these images... they are fucked. I'm sorry. I am. Even with everything your presence has put me through and the spoiled bitch you turned into, you don't deserve this. You shouldn't look, but you need to. I hope you aren't alone right now. I hope you have someone you can trust to help*

you through this because like I said... if you are watching this, I was wrong, and I am so sorry. I love you. I hate you. I wish things had been different. Be careful who you trust, sister. Things aren't always as they seem.'

The video disappears, and the images begin to flash across my laptop. Picture after picture of me... before Daddy... before Costin... before Jaxx and Abel and Joshua. I cover my mouth, trying not to vomit at the visual proof of the things my mother tried to set in motion with these photos. Slamming the laptop shut, I yank the drive from the USB port and throw it to the back of the closet and hug the photo and bracelet to my chest. I wasn't alone... I forgot... there were others. How could I just forget? What have I done?

Looking down at the blinking light on my phone, I pick it up and read.

Jonah: *I know you are, but I'm still here if you need a friend, beautiful. You aren't alone. The shadows can't touch you.*

Jonah: *Are you there?*

Missed call.

Jonah: *Pick up, beautiful.*

Missed call.

Jonah: *Please. Don't make me call Abel. I'm worried.*

My phone rings with another video call request. "Jonah?" I sob out.

"Eliana, where are you? Are you okay? What's going on? I'm arranging a direct flight to you right now." I can see him rushing through his hotel room in a panic.

"No, no, I'm okay. Stay." I shake my head vehemently.

"You're not okay, Eliana." He stops, and it feels like he can see directly into me, even from this distance. "You can't hide your shadows from someone who has seen them as closely as I have, beautiful. I can't help you from here, and it's killing me."

"Just a bad dream, rock star. Stay there. You have concerts all week, and I have my girls. I'm not alone. I just shut the door so I could talk to you privately without waking them. Not to mention, you will be here in a couple weeks, anyways. Thanks for the tickets by the way." I force a grin.

"Are you sure?" Jonah rubs his forehead

worriedly.

"I'm sure, but Jonah?" I sniffle, trying to hide the fact that inside I am in total ruins. "Can you sing to me? Something... happy?"

"For the girl who thinks I'm dreamy? Anything." He begins to sing, and I curl up on the closet floor, listening to him for what feels like hours until my tears have dried up and exhaustion wins out.

The next morning, I wake up to the sounds of Rachel ushering Nat and Isa from my room to catch their ride to the airport for a last hurrah before starting college... a freedom I will never have. I quickly tuck the photo into the back of my pants and clasp the bracelet around my wrist. Then I make my way into my room as if nothing has changed because I won't make them shoulder this, too. It's my burden to carry, alone.

CHAPTER THIRTEEN

Costin

Night after night, we watch. Night after night, we party. We wait. We play the roll we were groomed to fill. Finally, Douglass shows.

"How are you, Costin? Another beauty, I see." Douglass gestures at the dark hair bobbing in my lap. I fucking hate this part of the game. I don't want this girl, but it's all part of the show.

"Always." I laugh. "So, who did you bring tonight? Wouldn't mind taking someone new for a spin."

"Just you wait. They aren't on the menu, per se, but they put on one hell of a performance. I don't share, and the girl is still… intact." He laughs.

"Intact?"

"A virgin… technically, but you and I both know there are plenty of other ways to enjoy a body like that. They are both delicious." He nods in the direction of a beautiful young woman walking towards us, clinging to the hand of a lean, yet muscular guy. Both about my age and both scantily dressed. The kids from the photo.

Grinding my teeth, I take in a deep breath and attempt to tamp down my anger. They are adults now, but they have been with him for years. I can see it all in their eyes. How did this slip past us before? Have we always been so blind?

"Lilabelle. Kendrick. Show my friend Costin here what you can do. Dance for us." Douglass motions to the corner for the music to start. "Now."

Kendrick pulls her trembling body to his and whispers something into her hair then kisses her softly. Not sexually but comforting? Swaying to the music, they enchant the room with the most beautifully erotic dance I have ever seen. I have completely forgotten about the girl in my lap and knock her to the floor when I lean forward, watching only them. They are magic. Touching, caressing, and undressing each other as if they share one mind. Connected soul deep and only aware of each other, blocking out everything around them. I am in total awe until Douglass' shout breaks the trance.

"On your knees, both of you!" they quickly kneel at his feet as he frees his pathetic excuse for a cock. "Suck me. Together."

The man takes her hand, and they both lean forward, going to work on Douglass. After a few moments, he stands.

"Fuck her ass, Kendrick." Douglass demands, and a single tear rolls down her cheek.

"You're my girl, Lilabelle Fayre Maxfield. I am so sorry. You and me. Forever. I love you, Dame." Kendrick whispers with a trembling chin before kissing her.

"Maxfield?" My eyes go wide. No, it couldn't be. "Who-" but I am interrupted by shouts at the other end of the room.

Eliana

Night after night, I have sat alone. Night after night, I have nothing. No sunshine, no smiles, no laughter. Every emotion is painted on. My every move is faked. And I am done. In two days, I am set to wed Jaxx, and I have lost all hope of ever being free of my father's lies. The truth may set me free, but too many of them want me locked away. I miss my time with Jonah... I miss my life before and hate this life enough to take my chances with what comes after.

Sliding my foot into my red Jimmy Choo peep toe, I turn to the mirror, taking in the thin girl staring back at me. She is beautiful. She is flawless. She is a mirage. She is destruction and chaos. She is poison. She is the ruin of all that is good.

"Who are you?" I take another long drink from the bottle dangling at my side as a single tear rolls down my cheek.

"I hate you! It's all your fault!" I scream, throwing the heavy bottle at my trifold mirror and watching my reflection shatter before I crumble to the floor with a scream. The alcohol no longer dulls the pain. I am alone in my hell while everyone else moves on around me. The house is silent with the proof of that. I lean forward, picking up a large piece of broken mirror. I wonder if a girl without a beating heart can even bleed. Surely the blood no longer flows through my veins; it just sits stagnant as I am. I drag the rigid glass down my arm once, pausing when I hear laughter, and lean forward to glance out my window. Costin walks towards the kitchen door with his arm slung around yet another brunette. So it's a party night, great. He looks up at my window, and our eyes connect briefly before I turn away. I can't have him. Being with him is a betrayal to Joshua. So why shouldn't Costin have her? I told him to find better.

I don't even notice that I have dug the piece of glass deeper into my arm until I feel the warm blood dripping from my fingers. Fuck, looks like I do still bleed, but the giggling girl breaks the spell. Pissed off, I quickly grab a towel, wrap it around my arm, knotting it in place, and march from my room. Want to move on? Want to pretend that none of this has happened? Fine, but I am done letting them lock me away as if I don't exist while they party below my feet. The faithful fiancée. The obedient daughter. It's time they see what I've truly become. I'm already dressed for a night out. I guess the basement will do.

I walk into the main room and... gross... so many dicks. Old dicks, young dicks, fat dicks, thin dicks, lots of unimpressive dicks, and there are at least 3 girls for each one. This gets more disgusting every time. Holding my head high, I storm across the room, searching for the guys and growing colder with each step. This is what they left me for? *This* was more important than I was?

"Another one? Fuck this." A brunette pushes me from behind. "I am not competing with this prissy ass slut for Costin's attention. Andrew said he's mine tonight."

I turn, studying the girl, noticing our similarities. How often do they bring in girls that look like me?

"I said get out, skank!" She pushes me.

"Back the fuck up, bitch. Trust me, I wouldn't kneel for any of these dudes. He's yours. I just have some shit to handle, and I'm out." I stand my ground.

She steps back like she is going to leave but spins, spitting on the front of my three thousand dollar Dolce and Gabbana mini dress, then jumps at me, knocking us both to the floor. As soon as we hit the ground, I roll out from under her, straddling her hips and throwing fist after fist until her struggles have slowed to nothing more than whimpered begs. Don't start shit you can't handle, bitch.

Standing up, I look down on her with a curled lip. "Now we don't look anything alike. You're welcome."

Costin

"Who are-" I am interrupted by yelling at the other end of the room.

"Fuck!" Douglass yells as the girl clings to the man holding her. "There goes that. We're out of here. They don't perform in this kind of chaos. Call me when your shit is under control. Come on, we'll finish this at home." Douglass hands them both long coats and ushers them towards the stairs.

Before I can stop him, I hear Eliana's scream, and everything but her is immediately forgotten. I push through the crowd, quickly catching up with Jaxx and Abel running up from the subbasement where they were helping Andrew with an interrogation.

"Move!" I shout and freeze when I finally see her. No, not my Eliana. Not again.

Eliana

"Fucking move. Move!" I hear Costin yell as Jaxx and Abel help to push through the gathered crowd to get to me. I wanted to make them see me; here's my chance. Go big, or go home, Eliana. Reaching around to my back, I slowly pull down the zipper, allowing the straps of my dress to fall from my shoulders, sliding down my arms, pooling at my feet, and step out of it. "You ruined my dress, bitch. May as well use it to clean yourself up." I turn to my guys, who have frozen, and look each one in the eyes, refusing to be ignored another second. With my head held high, shoulders back, and wearing nothing but a tiny black thong, I own the room. "You're late, *again.*" Then, I turn, walking towards the stairs to the main floor, passing Richard on my way out, and causing him to choke on his drink. Great, Daddy will be thrilled.

"Munchkin, wait." Jaxx reaches for my arm, but I pull away, noticing Costin and Abel stayed behind. I know that the others can't follow me, but it still hurts. I want my family back. Our games have turned into reality. We aren't playing roles anymore, and there is nothing I can do to stop it.

"Baby, please? What happened? You're bleeding."

"Don't worry about it, Jaxx. Fuck knows none of you have spared me a single thought lately anyways." I shiver.

Pulling off his jacket, he covers me and smirks. "You have always been my priority; you know that. Did you really have to get naked? I'm sure the basement is buzzing over my fiancée now."

"Got your damn attention, didn't it? That's the thing, though, Jaxx. My whole life, you all told me how special I am, that I am worth more than an easy fuck. But when I needed you all the most, you showed me where I *really* ranked next to them.

Showed the whole room what your *fiancée* truly means to you." I stress the word fiancée mockingly and wipe away a tear that escapes. "I'm going back to my room. This was a bad idea, and she ruined my favorite dress. I was going to wear that to the next 3J concert to see Jonah." I stomp, and he flinches. Good.

"Come on, baby. I'm coming with you. I'm done for the night and planned on coming up shortly anyways." He leads me up to my room.

"Don't do that, Jaxx. I only want you with me if you want to be there, not because you feel guilty."

"Listen, there is nowhere else I would rather be." He closes the door behind us and reaches for me, trying to remove the jacket. "Hey, you're dripping blood."

"I'm fine. Besides, I'm naked under here." I step away, gesturing up and down my body.

"Trust me, I didn't forget," he rasps out. "However, I do need to get a look at that arm. Who knows what cut you. It could be-"

"I know what cut me, Jaxx. It's fine. I'm fine." I look at him. "I'm not fragile; I think I've proven that by now. Besides, there isn't anything left of me to hurt." I shrug. "I need a shower. I have tramp spit on me and who knows what else. Seriously, gross. Y'all nasty."

"Y'all? That's not my thing, baby. Never has been. Well, not since I left puberty behind." He brushes back his hair.

"It's not? Then, why are you down there? Why leave me up here alone?"

"Some things are best left unsaid, baby. I work for your dad. I go where he needs me, and that mess needs monitoring. Keeps them safe while they have fun, and I get to watch for other dangers."

"It's about me, isn't it?" He nods. "Why not tell me? Why just leave me here? All of you left me *again* and didn't even look back."

"There is nothing to tell that helps. It's all-" I hold up my hand, stopping him.

"Actually, Jaxx, I don't want to talk about it. It doesn't matter. I just want to shower and enjoy you being here for now. I don't want to spend the time I get with you angry. Find us something to watch? I'll be back."

I go into the bathroom and shut the door without waiting on an answer. If he does leave, I will actually fling myself from my bedroom window like I threatened to as a child.

I start the water, dropping his jacket and my thong to the floor. When I step inside, I run my hand through my hair, flinching when the warm water hits my open cut, causing Bethany's bracelet to wrap around some of the wet strands. I try gently untangling my hair from the delicate chain fighting through the burn in my arm, but the custom charm breaks free and hits the tiled floor with a resounding clink. Kneeling down, I ignore the fact that the water is tinted red and lift the tiny message from the floor, fighting back tears, and read the inscription. 'Love Remembers'... and I have been completely forgotten. Just like I forgot about *them*. My control shatters, and the emotions I have worked so hard to keep bottled up all hit me at once.

I smell Joshua as if he is in the room with me, close enough to feel but too far away to hold. His absence casts a constant darkness over my soul, and the guilt of still loving Costin through it all is eating me alive. Will it ever stop hurting? I collapse under the weight of my guilt, shatter from the pain of my losses, and I release my torment in a scream that reflects the never-ending suffering of my soul. Falling to the floor, I curl up in a ball and hold tight to my necklace, no longer caring enough to muffle my loud shuddering sobs.

"How does Iron Man sound- Baby, what's wrong?" Jaxx rushes into the shower, scooping me up in his arms and searching my face. "Talk to me."

"It hurts."

"What hurts? Your arm? Fuck, you're still bleeding!"

"Everything. Everything hurts, Jaxx. Make it stop. Please, help me. Make it stop. I can't... I can't breathe."

"What can I do, baby?"

"Make me forget, please. Just for a little while." I cling to him, pressing my bare chest to his wet shirt.

He studies me for a fraction of a second before nodding and lifting me from the floor. Walking us out of the bathroom, he grabs a towel from the sink as we go.

"Jaxx..." I beg, clinging to him desperately.

"I know, Munchkin. Hang tight; I've got you. I will always catch you." He carries me through my room, laying me softly on the bed, then unfolds the towel he grabbed from my vanity, leaning in to cover me. But I reach up, stopping him.

"Please, Jaxx, make me feel something other than pain. I can't take the loneliness anymore."

"I know, baby, but your arm needs bandages and your freezing. Let me take care of you, okay?" Jaxx asks, wrapping the plush towel around me. He rubs the chilled drops from my back and shoulders with even more tenderness than he did when I was a little girl running from our pool, shivering. Giggling through chattering teeth and nearly blue lips, I would dodge his attempts to care for me for as long as I could. Always launching myself into at least one more front flip back into the pool before he and Costin would manage to drag me in for a warm shower. I cling to that memory, mourning our long lost, carefree laughter.

I'm pulled from my thoughts when he kneels in front of me and opens the first-aid kit, taking my arm in his left hand.

"It's not as deep as it looked. I'm going to use the surgical glue, it will stop the bleeding faster." He frowns, gently cleaning the wound. "You did this to yourself, didn't you?"

"I did," I look away ashamed. "And I'm sorry. I was drinking, and I overreacted."

"You know I wouldn't survive losing you, right? None of us would." He pauses after applying the glue.

"I didn't want to die, I *don't* want to die. I just felt so alone. I don't know what I was thinking ..." I trail off.

"I am so sorry, Eliana. I should have been here." He stands and places a soft kiss on my forehead and crosses to his dresser. An obvious push from Daddy, our matching Blake Raffia dressers were a Band-Aid on the heart of a shallow princess, meant to distract and placate me because in this house, love means nothing when you have money.

I smile softly at Jaxx when he steps in front of me with a smirk, unfolding his found treasure and holding the shirt above my head. "Up."

"Hocus Pocus?" I lift my arms and shiver as he slides the threadbare fabric over my torso, the bottom edge coming to rest below my waist.

"You always did have a thing for the Sanderson sisters." He chuckles, stepping out of his wet clothing and into a pair of dry flannel pajama pants before sitting against the headboard, pulling my back into his chest, and resting his chin on my head.

I relax into him with a sigh, smiling as I read the faded text, 'Oh look another glorious morning. Makes me sick.'

"There's that smile," Jaxx says, poking a finger through a hole in the side of my t-shirt, and it hits me... What did I just do? I'm mortified... over my behavior and his rejection. I have to say something. I need to fix this.

"Jaxx, I-"

"Nope, it's time for you to listen, Munchkin. I know you hurt. I can't even imagine how broken you feel right now, but that-" He kisses my temple, gently rocking us side to side. "-was not the answer. Yes, I have always told you that you are better than that – that you are worth more – because it's true. You are no one's conquest. You are the most precious thing in my life, and I have spent years keeping you from being used and tossed aside like a worthless object. I'll be damned if I allow that now."

"Jaxx, you wouldn't have been using me." I sit up,

turning to face him. He would never.

"No. But are you in love with me, Eliana? Would you have been making love with me?" he questions sincerely.

"I do love you, Jaxx." I wipe away a tear.

"And I love you, Munchkin, but that's not how sex should be. Not for me and not for you. You should have better than a life settling for temporary physical pleasure. You deserve more. You had *more* with Joshua." I blush, looking away, and he tilts my chin to look him in the eyes. "Why would you ever allow yourself to settle for less than that again? Why would you want something skin deep when you know how it feels to give your entire heart and body to someone? How could that ever compare, and how could that take away the pain? Does it not just remind you of what it *should* be?"

"Jaxx I... I just..." I sob, falling into his chest. "I'm sorry, Jaxx. I just want it to stop. Something seemed better than nothing."

"Munchkin, when will you see that you have never really had nothing? You have me, Costin, Abel. We can't all be here and give you what you want, but you have our love. You have so much. It's just not the same as before. It never will be, and that's okay because one day, you will be ready to love again. That day, Eliana, you will look back and be so grateful that we didn't ruin what we have by covering up the memory of someone else. Don't taint our love with that." He brushes my hair from my face. "I'm not going anywhere. If you still want me later, once you have healed and you are truly ready, you can have me. I will always be here."

"You think it will get better, Jaxx? Really? Because I'm not too sure of that. The pain, it just grows every day. I feel like I am suffocating under the weight." I cry, pulling back slightly so I can look into his eyes when he answers me.

Pulling me into his chest, he cradles me, humming softly for a few moments until he speaks again. "I do, Eliana. Some pains are so deep, so consuming that you fight just to breathe every single day. They challenge your very soul. They are the real battles, not the ones out here against other people. The internal dragons are the hardest to beat. They are the ones that change you on a cellular level if you submit and the ones you have to *want* to slay in order to come out victorious. Eliana, you will win because I won't allow you to lose. I will continue to pick you up and dust you off for the rest of forever if I have to. I will follow you into the afterlife; don't test me. You are my world, Munchkin. You, Costin, and Abel are my family, but *you, Eliana, are my world.*"

"Jaxx, I am just so tired... it's all too heavy." I rub my chest.

"Then I will help you carry it, baby. Lean on me. I can be here. No red flags if I am with my fiancée. Lean on me. Share with me. I will fight *with* you."

"Okay." I nod, exhausted. I have a lot to think about... tomorrow. Especially the fact that I just tried to fuck Jaxx... yikes.

"Okay?" He raises a brow.

"Yeah. Read to me, Jaxx? Can we just pretend things are good again? That I'm still just the little girl who drives her hero insane and we have no worries other than breakfast cake and tiaras? For tonight?" I reach into the nightstand, removing the worn fairytales held together by a Champion's tape and a tiny girl's princess wishes, then hand it back to him, cuddling in under his arms.

"Hero, huh? Of course I will, Munchkin." He

tickles my side like he did when I was little and started wiggling too much, pulling a small giggle from me. He carefully opens the worn cover to the page marked by a pink velvet ribbon with a cupcake charm dangling from the bottom. Smiling down at the Eliana and Abel craft time creation from my childhood, Jaxx softly asks, "Now, where were we? Here?"

"Yeah, I love this part." I sigh, borrowing in under his arm. "Stay with me tonight?" I yawn.

"Nowhere I would rather be." He squeezes me tightly.

"Love you, Jaxx." I exhale.

"I love you, too, Munchkin…

'At last, the prince came to a chamber of gold where he saw upon a bed the fairest sight one ever beheld—a princess of about seventeen years who looked as if she had just fallen asleep. Trembling, the prince knelt beside her and awakened her with a kiss. And now the enchantment was broken. The princess looked at him with wondering eyes and said: "Is it you, my prince? I have waited for you long.'"

I drift off to sleep, listening to him read, remembering our before as he runs his fingers through my hair. In this moment, the weight on my heart seems lighter. I'm feeling a little less scared, a little less hopeless, and a little less alone. I take a deep breath, relaxing and thinking about everything that Jaxx has become for me over the years: family, protector, confidante, best friend, fiancée, and guiding light. He has saved me many times before, but tonight he saved me from myself in a way that no one else even took the time to notice. Tomorrow, we'll have to talk, but tonight I sleep soundly, wrapped in his arms.

Andrew

"What do you mean you lost them?!" I yell when Costin flops down on the couch beside me a few hours later. I had the room cleared after Poppet's little scene. Another moment I am really in awe of, but damn if she doesn't pick the most fucked up moments.

"I mean everything else slipped my mind when I heard E screaming. Can you blame me? With everything happening, we were afraid someone was... touching her," Costin says, pulling at his hair.

"You're sure they are the same couple? What did he call them?"

"Lilabelle and Kendrick. They were... close. Andrew, something is seriously wrong. We need to get them back here."

"I already have tons of requests for them. The dance left an impression. Douglass will bring them back. He will love the attention, especially if he has groomed them himself." I slam my tumbler on the table, feeling sick. There are monsters like me, and there are monsters like him. Neither of us deserves to breathe, but he deserves a special kind of death. A slow death. A painful death. I am the perfect kind of monster to give it to him, too.

"That's all you know? You said the boy called her Lilabelle Fayre Maxfield. That is oddly close to-" I start but notice Abel standing inside the doorway.

"It can't be. Costin, what did you see? What did you hear?!" Abel storms over to us, lifting Costin from the couch by the front of his shirt.

"Abel, I don't know. I don't know who she was. That's what I heard. Calm the fuck down!" Costin shouts, pulling away roughly.

"Fayre? Andrew, where did she go? You said she left! Where. Did. She. Go?!" Abel shakes with rage, and I stand. If this man snaps, I don't know if I can shoot him fast enough. He could kill me, I know it. He's loyal, but if he knows that I asked Richard to relocate *his* girl, he *will* kill me.

"Away, Abel. When she left here, she was very much alive. I told you that. She wanted out of this life, and I let her walk." I shrug... I mean, I did, kinda. Fuck if I knew where she went or-

"Was she pregnant, Andrew? Was that girl my...?" He doubles over like he's been physically struck.

"I don't know, Abel," I reply honestly. Back then, I didn't care. Not until it happened to me. Fuck.

"Wait, what's happening?" Costin stands beside us.

"The picture-" Abel pulls it from his pocket. "She looks just like Fayre, my ex-fiancée."

"Lil*abelle* Fayre *Maxfield. Abel Maxfield.* Holy

shit. She's your daughter." Costin goes white. "No wonder he didn't come to the other parties. *You* were here. But tonight, you worked below. He knows."

"We have to find her." Abel shakes me.

"We will find her. We'll find them both, and I want Douglass. He has some questions to answer."

"He's mine, Andrew," Abel hisses. "I am leaving. I'll find them."

"No, you can't, Abel. If he knows you are looking, we don't know what he could do," I tell him, and he snarls. If he finds Douglass first, he might find out I set this in motion. Unknowingly, but still. "Let me send a team. Jaxx can oversee it. There is a reason that Joshua wanted him on this. Let him do his fucking job. Let it sit until after the wedding. It's two days. He will relax, and that is when we will snatch him. You accompany Poppet later today, and we will throw Jaxx a bachelor party here... invite his dancers. We. Will. Get. Them."

"You protect my girl, Abel, and I will get yours," Costin promises.

"You better. Both of you." Abel turns, leaving the room. "Come on, Costin. We have a birthday to celebrate. I won't let her down, too."

They both leave the room, and I immediately start making calls. I will get them back here, and I will kill the motherfucker. Call it a warmup. This is going to lead me to the asshole after my daughter. Talk about two birds with one stone.

LOVE REMEMBERS

CHAPTER FOURTEEN

Costin

Grabbing her bags from my closet, I meet Abel outside her bedroom door. With everything they have planned for the wedding, I figured we could move up our normal gift routine to this morning. It might be tough to get her alone later, and I really need to see how she is *now*.

"Jaxx?" I look into his empty room.

"Must be with E." Abel motions to her room.

We step in yelling, "Happy birth-" and freeze.

"Oh, shit!" Abel turns away from the bed.

"OMG, knock. Would it kill you all to knock?" She shrieks, yanking the blankets over her head as Jaxx chuckles then stands and stretches.

"You motherfucking son of a bitch, I'll fucking gut you!" I storm towards him, but Abel blocks my path.

"That's going to have to wait, Costin," Jaxx replies calmly, blocking her from view and pulling back the blanket, whispering something to her.

"Jaxxson?" Abel rubs his neck.

"What the fuck, man?"

"It's nothing-" Jaxx is interrupted

"Drop it guys," She stands from the bed, wearing his shirt which stops right below her knees and is nearly see-through. "I was a mess and made a damn fool of myself. Plus, neither of you cared two shits about me last night, so why even ask now?"

Jaxx's head snaps to her, and his jaw tenses. "Baby, you didn't-" she holds up a hand, shaking her head.

"I begged him to take me to bed, and he turned me down, so just let it fucking go. *He* didn't do anything. I did. Pathetic, huh?" She snorts, walking to her bathroom and placing a hand on the knob. She glances at her bandaged arm and then looks back at the three of us.

"I needed help. I'm sorry. I just... it was too dark in here." She rubs her chest absently. "So don't yell at him. I'm not something fragile you need to protect... not anymore. I'm just trying to survive long enough to set things right. Just like I told Jaxx last night." She looks at me, ignoring her tears, exposing the depth of her pain, and taking me down with her. "There was no risk to me, nothing left to damage. You can't break something that has already been demolished. All that's left to do is wade through the rubble. Thank you for being there for me, Jaxx. I'm sorry I put you in that kind of position."

She shuts and locks the bathroom door behind her as we stare at the now empty space. Jaxx moves first, rushing toward the door, ready to tear it down.

"Whoa, Jaxx, wait. What happened? Give her a minute, and talk to us," Abel says.

"Fuck you both! I thought I got through to her last night when we talked, but you had to come in here, insinuating things, and she shut down… again," he roars, brushing the hair from his face. "What happened? After she left the basement, I brought her up here to watch a movie, to try to calm her down. She said she wanted to shower, but not three minutes later, I heard her sobbing. I went in to check on her and found her curled in a ball under the bench, ice-cold. I picked her up to get her out of the cold water, and she looked at me as if I had all of the answers. Like I could put her back together. She wanted me to take away her pain. I couldn't do it. I just couldn't use her like that even if she was asking for it. She is still too fragile; how could I? So we talked. I tried to take care of her heart, and then she fell asleep to me reading to her just like she used to… before. Peacefully. "

"And we're supposed to believe that shit?" I spit.

"Fuck you, Costin. Where were you when she was breaking?" Guilt assaults me because we all know were Abel and I were. Where we always are. With fucking Andrew.

"What you all asked me to do because I fucking love her!" I bellow.

"Quiet down, both of you." Abel glances at the

bathroom door.

"Get out. Let me talk to her for a minute, and I'll be down. We have to end things now. I want answers. I can't watch her self-destruct like that again. We have to bring her back to us, and this is the only way," Jaxx huffs, pushing back his hair.

"You don't even know the half of it. I need your help, but I am going to need you focused. So go take care of her first." Abel motions to the bathroom.

"This is fucked, Jaxx." I turn for the door but change course when I see the shattered mirror and dried blood on the carpet. Dropping to my knees, I lift a large piece of blood-covered glass.

"Jaxx, what *else* happened last night?" Abel steps over to us.

"Her arm?" I look up to Jaxx, and he gives a single nod.

"Her darkest demons and her very rock bottom. That's the Eliana I tried to save last night. Now, tell me either of you would have turned her away." Jaxx walks back to the bathroom door. "I need to talk to her. She thinks-" He shakes his head. "I need to talk to her." He pulls out a key, unlocking the door, and walks in, sealing us on the outside.

I hate him for this, but I love him for it, too. She hurt herself while we were balls deep in coke and whores, again. He is the better man.

"He's in love with her too, Cos."

"Fuck that. I would have known."

"I've said it before, and I'll say it again... you are a damn fool sometimes. You really need to open your eyes. When it comes to E, you are fucking blind." Abel offers me a hand up.

"Bullshit." I stand, turning to leave, but stop to pick up a photo from the floor. "Where the hell did this come from?"

"What?" Abel looks over my shoulder, "I haven't seen that one before. Bethany and E were what, eleven?"

"Ten, I remember that Christmas. She nearly poisoned me with those damn cookies."

"Ornaments, Cos. You weren't supposed to eat them." Abel rolls his eyes. "Anyways, put it up. The last thing she needs is something else upsetting her. Meet me downstairs once you are done. We have a lot of fucking work to do."

"Yep," I walk into her closet, looking for her box of photos, but a small purple zip drive catches my attention. "What the fuck is this?"

Eliana

I'm stepping out of the shower when I hear the bathroom door click shut, and I'm immediately on high alert until I feel Jaxx's arms wrap around my waist from behind.

"I really am sorry, Jaxx." I lean into him, avoiding his gaze in the mirror.

"Look at me, baby. Look." He turns me to him, lifting me onto the counter, and steps between my parted thighs. Tilting my chin up with his index finger, he softly kisses my nose as he continues smiling. "There is nothing to apologize for. You didn't do anything wrong. If I was a weaker man, things would have gone much differently."

"Oh yeah? How is that?" I laugh, rolling my eyes. "Running from the room, screaming because there was a disgusting, clearly insane woman begging for you to bang the sad out of her?"

"Oh, for fucks sake," he laughs, hugging me close to him. "You have to know that me not making love to you had *nothing* to do with your looks, right?"

I hold him close, breathing deeply. "Honestly, Jaxx? I don't know anything anymore. I haven't been sure of who I am in quite some time."

"Eliana, I didn't make love to you because it wasn't the right thing to do. It's not what you really need. You need love. You need a partner. You don't need to be used and tossed to the side. You have to see that, right? How would you feel right now if we had gone through with things last night?"

I look away, knowing he is right. "I just wish..." I avert my gaze.

"Tell me." He smiles softly, turning my face back to his.

I release a sigh. "Things are so tangled, Jaxx. Joshua is-" I fight back tears. "-gone. Costin was never an option. Even when he was, he wasn't. Doesn't matter how I feel about him. Not after everything. You have been pushed into marrying me even though you aren't in love with me." I let out a small sob, continuing before he has a chance to make it all seem okay. We're losing. No matter how he spins it, we've lost so far. "The wedding is tomorrow, and holy fuck, today is my birthday!"

"It is, baby." He smiles. "And the wedding? It's no sacrifice on my part. I do love you. You're my person, too. Joshua wanted you safe and happy. I will never let anyone hurt you ever again. As for happy... would a life as my wife be so bad, Eliana?"

"No, but-" I'm interrupted by the bathroom door swinging open, smacking the wall. I shriek as Jaxx takes a defensive stance in front of me.

"Get off Jaxx's dick and come with us, bride!" Isa marches in.

"Costin said to let ourselves in, and hellooo...." Nat takes in Jaxx, eyes widening as she stares at his chest. I giggle when he spins back to face me in an attempt to hide, only cursing softly when he realizes his movements caused my towel to slightly pull apart. Maybe he was being honest when he said that him turning me down had nothing to do with my looks.

"Well, at least the mystery of why you quit fucking Jonah has been solved." Jaxx growls as Nat makes a beeline for the makeup case beside me, remarking, "Jaxx, buddy, no reason to hide a body like that."

"Should really put it on display... a work of

fucking art." Isa offers me a high-five that I reluctantly return just so she will stop.

"Oh, that note," Jaxx growls, carrying me into my room, kicking the door closed and leaving them in the bathroom. Setting me on my feet, he looks down at me. "I needed out of there. Are they always like that?" I grin and shrug... yeah... they are. "Comforting, E. Get dressed. You have plans with those harlots. Feeling great about your bachelorette party now?" He laughs, pressing his lips to my temple.

"Where are you going?" I ask him since he's dressing quickly and tucking his Glock into the back of his slacks.

"I should really get one of those." I gesture to his sidearm.

"A gun?" He raises a brow.

"Yep." I smile.

"Nope. Work. I need to make sure everything is secure for tomorrow and maybe get you some solid answers as another wedding gift," he offers, looking away, obviously hiding something.

"Jaxx, you don't have to marry me, you know?" He stalks over, pulling me into a tight hug.

"It's not that, baby. I just feel like I've failed you. I know where your heart lies, and I promise we will work this out. But for now-" He walks quickly to the door, glancing to the closet and back to the bathroom. "- get dressed. Come on ladies. Last minute run-through before heading out."

"See ya downstairs, Lili." They follow Jaxx out, shutting the door behind them.

"Every man in this house is insane," I say to myself as I walk into my closet to dress, dropping my towel right before I feel him.

"Costin?" I turn, whimpering when I notice his rapid breathing and lust filled eyes. "What are you doing here? Jaxx... the wedding."

Costin

"You don't think he noticed me slip in here?" I ask, not taking my eyes from her body while slipping the drive discreetly into my pocket. She is even more beautiful than I thought she would be. "Princess, you're fucking gorgeous. I..."

She releases a small moan when I lick my lips

and adjust myself. Meeting her gaze, I step forward with a growl. Mine. "Fuck it, you aren't married yet." I pull her to me, and she jumps, wrapping her legs tightly around my waist. Kissing her deeply, I spin, pinning her to the wall. Knowing I won't be able to hold back, I warn her. "This is gonna be fast and hard. I don't think I can control myself, not with you. Are you ready for me, Eliana?"

She nods, reaching between us, and pushes down the elastic waist of my sweats then bites my shoulder to muffle her scream when I immediately slam my cock inside her.

"Shh. They'll hear you, Princess." I chuckle, pulling back and slamming into her again. I grip her hips, no doubt leaving small bruises, while thrusting into her repeatedly. With her back pressed to the wall, she takes every fucking inch of my cock. I pound into her relentlessly, enjoying every second I am inside her like it's my last. It probably will be. I can't believe Jaxx turned a blind eye this time. For her.

"Time to cum for me, baby."

"I... I..." she pants, clawing my back and shaking her head. "It's too much. I can't."

"Oh yeah? What if I-" Slowing, I begin circling my hips, grinding into her and adding new friction to her already sensitive clit. I chuckle when her legs tighten around my waist, encouraging me to pick up the pace. "Thought so. Let go for me, Princess. I need to feel you cum all over my dick."

"Oh, Costin. Fuck." Her legs begin to tremble, and when I roll her nipples between my fingers, she fucking explodes, tightening around me and pulling me over the edge with her.

Sealing my mouth over hers, I swallow her screams as my cock swells and fucking fills her.

"God, Princess." I still, leaning my forehead to hers. "Mine. I love you so fucking much. Run with me. *Be* with me, Princess."

She looks behind me at the small rack of Jaxx's clothing, going white, and sobs. "Oh, my God, what have I done? I'm so sorry." She wiggles free and ducks under my arm in an attempt to leave.

"Princess, please don't." I grab her hips, pulling her back to me.

"No, I-" She stiffens, pivoting and pushing me behind her wall of gowns when she hears her door open and footsteps approaching the closet.

"I don't care Jaxx. It's fucked for you two to do this to her." Abel swings the door open as she pulls a dress from her left, stepping into it. "You all right, Darlin'? Where the hell is he?"

I step back out, pulling at my hair as she grabs her purse and rushes from the room in tears.

Abel curses, watching her go. "You were supposed to put away the photo so she didn't get upset."

"I did."

"Yeah, I mean fucking her the night before her wedding didn't upset her worse than the photo would have." Abel snorts with disgust as Jaxx's face falls. Then, he turns quickly, walking after her.

"Maybe, but we are still in love with each other whether she can admit it while sober or not. She can't fight it forever, and she just proved that to us both. She felt what I felt. I saw it in her eyes." I sigh. "She was willingly mine for a moment, and I don't regret a single second."

CHAPTER FIFTEEN

Eliana

Rushing down the stairs, I blow past Daddy with a quick peck on the cheek and hurry to the car where the girls are waiting.

"Poppet, we need to talk about last night. "

"No, we don't, Daddy. Super busy... wedding... adulting... gotta go."

"Eliana. Stop." I stumble when I hear Jaxx call

after me but right my footing and practically launch myself into the back of our limo. "Get in!" I hiss at the girls when they refuse to move.

"Excuse us." Jaxx steps in, shutting the door with them still outside.

"Traitors," I whisper looking away.

"Baby, talk to me."

"You knew. Were you setting me up?" I pull back, closing off my emotions and wrapping my arms around myself. "Why?"

"You love him. I wanted you to remember how *that* feels. Remember the difference. " He reaches for my hand.

"I love Joshua," I defend.

"Joshua is dead, baby. He's not coming back." He wipes a tear from my cheek, sucking it from his thumb just as Charming had done the day I met him, and I sob. Pulling me onto his lap, Jaxx holds me while I try to compose myself.

"I was supposed to marry *him* tomorrow. I love you Jaxx, but at least with you, it's survival. We aren't engaged because we are head over heels in love, Jaxx. We are doing what we have to do. Costin is different, though; he's a betrayal to everything I had with Joshua. The only man my Charming feared I loved more than him, and now I feel like I have tainted that love and disrespected you, all in one impulsive moment. I am garbage. I don't deserve you. Joshua would be disgusted with me if he were here," I cry.

"God, baby, I didn't think you would feel that way. I honestly thought I was helping you. I wanted you to see that you can be happy with me without giving him up again. You can have both safety and be in love." He holds me close. "You do deserve me, and you are crazy if you think Joshua would be disgusted. He loved you so much. If the roles were reversed-" He shivers, squeezing me tighter, kissing my temple. "-he would be just as lost as you are, baby."

"I'm sorry, Jaxx." I scoot in close, hugging him around the waist. "It won't happen again. I promise I can be a good wife. You're right; our life won't be a bad one."

"There is nothing to be sorry for. It's my fault. We will work this out later. Your heart, it matters, baby. Never say never." He places a soft kiss on the corner of my mouth. "Now, go have fun with your friends.

Regular fun, not that man displaying, penis eating kind of fun."

"Okay," I laugh. "I'll see you... when?"

"When you get back." He chuckles, stepping from the car. "I'll be the one in the tux."

"The one in the tux..." I nod slowly. "Holy shit."

"Yes, holy shit." He smiles back. "Be careful, Eliana. Smart choices. Stay alert and together. The area has been cleared and is being patrolled, but sometimes..."

"Sometimes, things happen anyways," I whisper. "I will Jaxx. Love you."

"I love you, too, baby." He steps back, letting the girls climb in. Abel gets in the front, allowing us some privacy, knowing I need it right now. The second we are alone and the driver pulls away, they both start in.

"What was that?" Nat yells.

"Which one did ya fuck?!" Isa squeals.

"Costin." I bury my face in my hands. "I'm an emotional mess."

"Wedding is still on?" Nat scoots up to me, lifting my head and wiping my tears, then begins applying my makeup.

"Yeah, still on." I nod as Isa brushes my hair.

"Can you get away with fucking a rock star today, too?" Isa asks, teasing my roots.

"Can I what? No! Why are you the way that you are?" I snort out, missing Charming even more in this moment, knowing they will both miss my The Office reference.

"All done!" Isa declares as we pull up to the swanky oceanfront resort.

"Wow." I stand from the limo, stretching, and breathe in deeply. I needed this. It's new, and there are no memories connected to this place. This moment in time belongs to us. Free.

"Okay, let's get you ladies settled."

Once Abel has cleared our room, he pulls me to the side.

"Darlin', I..." I rush to him, hugging him tightly.

"I love you, big guy." I look up at him, smiling.

"I love you, too. Now, just have fun. Tonight is *yours*. You *are* free tonight. I can't do much, but whatever happens in this room stays in this room. Got it? You are safe, so just... breathe... and dance." He laughs.

"Hell yeah," I hoot.

Hours later, we are in our bikinis, dancing around the room, drunk. Stepping onto the bed, I begin jumping as I belt out Truth Hurts, realizing I haven't felt this free since-

"Room for one more?" I choke, hearing his familiar voice.

"Jonah?" I turn, screaming. "Oh my God! It *is* you! What are you... Oh, no, nope. Can't do that! I promised, and I am a bittle drink a lit." I giggle. "Wait, that's not right."

"Shh, just shut up and dance with me, beautiful." He grins, jumping to the floor and reaching out for me. Shrugging, I launch myself into his arms, nearly knocking him off his feet. Once he rights us, we begin dancing. "When you sober up a bit, we're gonna talk."

"Shh, no talky." I laugh, pressing a finger to his lips.

"Okay, no talky." He pulls me to him, pushing a bottle of water into my hands. "Drinky."

Ten songs and three bottles of water later, I follow him onto the deck, putting my arms on the railing and looking out at the water.

"Feeling better?" He leans against the rails

beside me, watching the ocean roll in and out.

"Yeah... Have you ever been jealous of the waves, Jonah?"

He turns to me, puzzled. "No, why would I be?"

"When I was younger, my father used to tell me how dangerous the water was. I can still hear him laughing at my fear of the waves while trying to warn me of the real dangers below the surface. 'The waves are simply the ocean dancing, Princess. The real danger is what you can't see, so never go in alone. The currents will pull you under and turn you around until you have no idea which way is up.'" I smile at Jonah, wiping away a stray tear.

"He's a smart man." Jonah nods.

"Yes, he *was*. See, those waves are the most carefree part of the water. No matter how hard the ocean tries to pull them back in, to break them of their dance... their *freedom*... it can't. Those waves-" I motion to the water, whispering. "-are everything I try to be. What's not to envy, Jonah? Their spirit? Their strength?" Wiping away another tear, I look into his eyes, my voice breaking. "The currents are winning, Jonah. They have pulled me under, and I am *drowning*."

"Eliana." He huffs out my name as if he's been punched.

"I wanna be a wave, Jonah."

"Then let's be waves, beautiful." He takes my hand.

"Things are different now." We both look at my ring.

"A current?" he asks.

"No, he's drowning, too. He just won't admit it."

"Are you in love with him?"

"It doesn't matter." I smile, stepping off the deck and wiggling my toes in the sand. "If I can't be a wave, then at least we can dance with them." I grin up at Jonah and then sprint down the sand into the water, screaming when the first wave rushes over my feet.

"It's three a.m.! You'll freeze." Jonah sweeps me up, trying to carry me back to the dry sand when an unexpected surge of water knocks us over.

"Holy shit, that's cold," he yells out, and I laugh.

"You feel that, Jonah?"

"The cold? Yeah I feel it." He scoops me into his arms and carries my shivering body up the shore, placing me on a lounge, and runs up to grab the blanket from the deck. Sitting behind me, he pulls my back to his chest and wraps the blanket around us both.

"That, Jonah, was a wave trying to remind me who I am." I lean into him, shivering, slowly warming back up as my eyes begin to get heavy.

"And who is that, beautiful?"

"I am Eliana Annalise Jameson, and I am a hell of a lot stronger than the woman I have allowed myself to become."

"Yeah, and what are you going to do about that?" I can hear the smile in his voice.

"I'm going to fight back." I drift off but whisper, "Thank you for being my friend tonight, Jonah."

"Thank you for letting me." He rubs my arm.

"Will you sing for me?"

"Whatever you need, beautiful," he replies, resting his head atop mine, softly singing a song I've never heard before as I fall asleep.

"When the shadows start to creep back in and the darkness haunts your dreams, you simply have to say my name. I would walk through hell to pull you back to me..."

LOVE REMEMBERS

CHAPTER SIXTEEN

Costin

"Well that was a fucking bust." I sigh, dropping down onto the couch in the basement once the room has finally cleared. "I'm going to crash for an hour or so before we have to start getting ready."

"Yeah, me too." Jaxx runs his hand through his hair, sitting in the chair across from me. "I really thought Douglass would show, Cos. I don't know how I am going to tell Abel. What will I say to Eliana? We are getting married today, and then I am immediately going to head out to search for the girl. Happy honeymoon, baby. No, I can't tell you where I am going or when I will be back. Is it safe? Well..."

"Fuck you, Jaxx. Get the hell out!" I stand quickly, overwhelmed with jealousy, shoving him from the chair. "At least you get to be with her! You know what this is like for *me?* I get to watch her get married to a man she isn't even in love with while I sit to the side, pretending to be the man-whore they expect me to be. Every time I have to touch another woman, I want to puke."

"Fuck *me*, brother?" he chokes out. "You know what it's like to be the man that loves her, knowing she doesn't love you in return? Do you know what it's like to look into the eyes of the girl that owns your entire heart and hear her call you her *very best friend*? To see your ring on her finger and know that it means nothing to her but *everything* to you. To hold her in your arms at night and then give her to the man you call your brother the very next day? Wrecking your own heart continuously because no matter what *you* feel, her heart comes first every time. So, *brother*, tell me more about *your* suffering. Because, no matter what else is going on, *she loves you back*."

"It changes nothing. She isn't with me. She is with you. At least, you have that." I spit.

"It changes *everything*, Costin! Damn it!" He shoves me to the floor. "She loves *you*! What I wouldn't give to be where you are right now! Can't you see what you have? Stop being a child, and *look*. You. Have. Her. Heart. You have everything. Can't you just be patient with her? Isn't she worth it?"

"She's worth everything, Jaxx. I didn't realize-" I stand and freeze when I hear something drop to the floor from my pocket. "Fuck."

"What is that, Costin?" Jaxx picks up the purple drive from the floor, turning it over in his hand.

"How could I have forgotten? I found that in her closet this afternoon when..."

"Yeah, I remember, thanks. What *is* it?" Jaxx huffs.

"I don't know, but I snuck it into my pocket. I figured it was worth a look. I didn't want to ask her just in case..." Jaxx nods, understanding my reasoning.

"I know. Grab that laptop, no time like the present."

Eliana

"Time to go, Darlin,'"

"Go away, Abel. Sleeping," I groan smacking Abel away.

"Is this you fighting back?" Jonah laughs under me.

"Holy shit. Today is-"

"Your wedding day." Abel pulls me to my feet.

"Holy shit!" I spin. "Are you coming, Jonah?"

"Am I welcome?" He laughs nervously.

"Should probably show up with the other guests, man." Abel slaps him on the shoulder.

"I'll be there. You're sure you want to go through with it? Can still leave with me." He grins.

"I won't leave them to drown alone, rock star." I hug him. "See you in a couple hours?"

"Yep."

Arriving home, I head straight up to Jaxx's room but turn when I hear Joshua's voice from my room across the hall. Running in, I throw open the door and freeze.

It's complete chaos. The beautiful castle canopy around my bed is hanging in shreds; broken lanterns and strands of lights flicker, casting a haunting light across the devastation, and photos of me blanket every surface and wall. Joshua and me. Costin and me. Me and Jonah... Abel... Jaxx...I gasp when I hear him again... us... playing from a broken laptop laying in the middle of the room. I watch it happen all over again.

"No, Angel, no. Don't you say goodbye," he begs.

"Tell me you love me, Charming."

"With every single beat, Angel. In this life and the next, for all of eternity."

"Every single beat, even in the next."

I sob, turning to run from the room. Stumbling and crashing into a broad chest, I feel a pinch in my neck.

"I got tired of waiting, Eliana. You're *not* marrying him." I look up into a set of eyes I have known most of my life. A set of eyes belonging to a man I trusted. Lifting me as my legs go weak, he says, "Rest now. I've got you."

With the last of my strength, I breathe out, "Why?"

"Because you belong to me, sweet girl." He chuckles, and I sleep.

Costin

We walk to the desk in the far corner and plug in the drive.

"'Watch first.' Costin, I have a really bad feeling about this. There are hundreds of image files here." He clicks play on the video, and I want to scream when I hear what Bethany has to say. How could she? Has Eliana watched this?

'Okay, so I don't even know why I am doing this... images... they are fucked... shouldn't look...need to...I hope you aren't alone right now... help you through this... I love you. I hate you...Be careful who you trust, sister. Things aren't always as they seem.'

Then... the images start.

"*Fuuuck!*" Jaxx screams. "Has she watched this? Did she know?"

Image after image flashes across the screen. I

can't look away. I want to. I *need* to, but I can't. What if there is something there? What if *he* is there?

"What the fuck is that?" Andrew steps into my room, marching over to the desk and slamming his hand down beside the computer. "Where did that come from?"

"Andrew, I-"

"Freeze it." Jaxx barks from behind me. "It's them. Isn't it?"

"They were there in the basement with her? Where were they when we found her?" Andrew asks with a furrowed brow.

"That-" Jaxx points to the screen. "-three shadows... Puckett? Smaller one must be female. But the other? Who is *that?*"

Our conversation pauses when Jaxx's phone rings.

"Abel, not now. Take her up to her room... Abel? *Abel?!*" He puts the phone on speaker, and my heart stops.

"Ja... rd ha..." Bang! "uck!... out... now...elp!" we run for the stairs, knowing that we won't be able to hear him until we are on the main floor. The added walls and sound proofing are great for security but shit for cell phones. By the time we reach the main floor, the call is silent.

"Abel!" Jaxx shouts into the phone, and we all run into the yard, pushing through caterers, planners, and event staff. Where is fucking security?

"You all look out here!" I yell back, heading up to her room. When I get there, I have to grip the door to keep from collapsing. One of our guys and the two women sent to get E ready for the wedding are laying dead by the bathroom door, and her room is trashed. Photos blanket every surface, and a video is playing on loop, of the night Laporte was murdered, in the center of the floor.

I rush through the destruction to turn off the heart wrenching cries coming from the laptop and hoping to find something, anything. Her heart shaped pendant, our connection, our biggest chance of finding her, is hanging from the corner of the shattered screen. Her distorted, tear stained face stares back at me, and I collapse.

"Nooo!"

"Costin! What happened... no," Jaxx wheezes, taking in the room. The bed we bought our tiny girl is now in shreds. "No. No, no, no, no. Not again. No."

he grabs his head, tears running down his cheeks.

"Andrew!" I yell, standing and pulling Jaxx to face me, looking into his eyes. This time, I will be the one to lend him strength. I am breaking too, but he is right. It is time for me to man up. For her.

"Jaxx." I shake him. "We are going to find her. We always do. Focus. This is what you do. We raised her and trained her. She is a survivor. A fighter. And we are her always. We *will* find her."

His eyes harden, and I can see the cold running through his veins. "I will kill every fucking one of them. Yes, we will find her, and we will eliminate every single threat. Today, their blood will pool at my feet, brother. Let's go."

CHAPTER SEVENTEEN

Eliana

"You need to wake up, Angel." I hear his voice, but it's so dark.

"Joshua?"

"You need to wake up and run. You're not safe! Wake up! Now!"

I jolt awake... a dream? Where am I? Why can't I move?

"There she is." Richard strolls towards me, grinning when he sees me tug at my restraints. "Sorry about that, sweet girl. Needed to make sure you wouldn't run before I had a chance to explain everything."

"Explain what? Why am I here? Where are the guys? Jaxx? Daddy?"

His lip curls in disgust as his eyes go dark, and he roughly grabs my face in his left hand, squeezing.

"Those fucking fools are still chasing their tails. They won't even notice you are gone until the music plays for no bride." He chuckles then shrugs. "I really expected them to be smarter. If it wasn't for you, I would have killed them all and walked away years ago."

"For me? Why would you wait for me?"

Running a hand down my body, he pauses when he reaches the hem of my swim cover-up, flipping it with a flick of his wrist, exposing my body in nothing but the string bikini I wore home from the resort after oversleeping on the beach with Jonah. When he runs a finger up my inner thigh, crossing to the other, I scream, struggling against the restraints holding me to the bed.

He places a hand over my mouth. "Now look what you've done. You've woken our guest." I still when I hear the muffled yells from the next room, and he moves his hand from my mouth to my throat, giving it a gentle squeeze as he smiles darkly.

"What guest, Richard? Who else is here?" I ask, keeping my voice steady. I won't fail this time. Whoever is in there *will* live.

"That caveman that follows you everywhere." Oh, God, he has Abel. "I was going to kill him, but I remembered that we will need a witness, and you would be less than happy with me for spilling his blood all over the beach house."

"A witness for what, Richard?" my blood freezes when he turns to my white dress hanging in the corner. "Why? Why me?"

"Because you're mine, sweet girl." He leans forward, kissing me, but I bite down when I feel his tongue push its way into my mouth. He spits. "So be it. Guess we're going to have to find another witness."

He turns to walk from the room when I yell, "Wait! I'll do it. I'm sorry. I was just scared." I default to the helpless act, hoping he'll buy it.

"You will?" He arches a brow, unconvinced.

"The restraints." My chin trembles as a tear falls from my eye. "I thought you were going to hurt me. I saw pictures from Puckett, and I thought-"

"No, absolutely not." He runs a hand down my cheek, and I force myself not to pull away. "I love you. I'm not a sick pervert like they were. I waited for you. You're a woman now. If I let you out, you have to promise to do as I say. If you don't, if you run, I *will* kill him. Understood?"

"Yes, sir." I tremble, earning me a smile from him, and he goes to work, freeing me. Of course, he would like that. Gross.

Helping me to stand, he pulls my body against his, "Better?"

"Much," I whimper.

"I can't wait. I want you now." He leans to kiss me, but I interrupt him.

"Please, can I check on Abel? I won't be able to focus on us-" I could puke. "-if I don't know he's okay." Richard looks angry, but I explain. "He's my family, Richard. My big brother."

"Your brother. Well I must apologize now

because your *brother* put up one hell of a fight. I had to shoot him." He shrugs, chuckling.

"You what?!" I shriek. Who just shoots another person like it's nothing?

"Calm down, sweet girl. It's just a leg. I do love that temper, though." He smirks, laughing aloud at my wide eyed expression.

"Just a- for fucks sake. Take me to him," I huff out, exasperated. I know I should be playing this sweeter, but seriously? Plus, he seems entertained by me. When he arches a brow, I pout. "Please?"

Amused, he shakes his head, running his thumb over my bottom lip. "How could I say no to those lips? We have to hurry. I need to feel them around my cock."

Shit. Yes, he's hot, but he's old enough to be my father, and he's clearly insane. How had we not seen this before?

Taking my hand, he leads me into the living room where Abel lays, bound at the arms and legs, on a blood soaked carpet.

Rushing to his side, I cry out. "Abel? Abel, talk to me. Please, be okay." He grunts, and I pull the tape from his mouth.

"Run," he whispers.

"Never." I stare into his eyes. "I will *never* abandon you. You know better."

"Darlin', please."

"No," I hiss and then turn, knowing exactly how to get what I need from a man like Richard even if it will cost me later. Widening my eyes in vulnerable desperation and feeding into his ego, I beg. "Please, baby, get me something to help him. Don't let him die."

Sighing, he smiles down at me. "Okay, sweet girl, but what do I get?"

"Huh?" I play dumb. "What do you mean?"

"You, I want you, Eliana. Today. Here." He points to the couch to our right.

"Fuck that. No. Absolutely not. No!" Abel yells, fighting against his ties.

"Please calm down," I whisper, placing a hand on his face, but startle when I hear Richard stomping toward us.

"I fucking warned him to keep quiet!"

"No!" I scream when he pulls back his leg to kick. I quickly place myself between his approaching foot and Abel, and everything goes black when his shoe connects with the back of my head.

"*Wake up. You have to get away, Angel.*" Another soft whisper as a sweet breath fans across my face. "*Wake up!*"

Slowly blinking awake, I attempt to shake away the fog and remember what happened. I am startled at how desperate Richard looks, stomping back and forth, yanking at his hair. How long was I out? Eyes connecting with mine, he rushes to my side.

"My God! Are you okay? Why would you do that?" He shakes me, rattling my already aching head.

"Abel?" I need to see that he's okay.

"He's fine, see? Good as new. I even fixed him up for you." I look over to see Abel secured to a chair with a white cloth tied tightly around his leg.

"Thank you," I whisper.

"You okay, Darlin'?" Abel rasps.

"Yeah, Abel. I'm good."

"It's time. Sign this, sweet girl!" Richard claps.

"Sign what?" I look down, gasping at the already notarized marriage license. "How did you-"

"It's amazing the kinds of favors you gather as a lawyer, especially when ninety percent of your clients have things to hide." He grins, wiping a white residue from his nose.

"This can't be legal." How high is he?

"I assure you it is, Eliana, and you will sign it. Now. See-" He leans over, signing his name to the document. "Now you. Do it, or he dies." He points to Abel.

"Darlin'-"

"Shut your fucking mouth and watch!" he snarls then smiles at me. "You want to, don't you, sweet girl?"

"Yes, yes I do." I lean forward, signing. There's no way this will hold up, but I won't resist. He's insane, stoned, and seems to have reached the end of his rope. Fighting this would be too much of a risk.... Just wait.

He shoves a ring into my hand.

"With this ring I thee wed." He slides a ring onto my finger. The fuck is this mess? He holds out his hand. "Now you!"

"Okay..." I put the ring he handed me on his finger. "With this ring I thee wed?"

"Fuck yea, you do." He pulls me in, roughly kissing me, but Abel curses. "I'm shooting him. I'm not listening to this shit on our wedding night."

"Or! Why don't we go to the bedroom? Light some candles? I can do that thing you wanted?" I shoot Abel a look that screams shut up when Richard glances in the direction of the bedroom. God help me, I have to get us out of here.

"Yeah, we can do that. Let's go." He pulls me from the room quickly as I stumble over my feet, trying to keep up with his wide strides.

Entering the bedroom, I quickly take in my surroundings, noticing his cell phone on the table beside the bed. I need to get to that phone.

"Richard, can I have a moment to… prepare. I look a mess and want to look perfect for our first time." I trail a finger down his bare chest, stopping when it lands on his belt buckle.

"You have three minutes, and then you're mine, wife." He breathes in, leaning forward and kissing me roughly, moaning deeply, and grinding his hips against me.

"Three minutes." I bat my lashes, stepping back.

He grabs his cock through his pants, smiling darkly, and strides from the room. Pausing in the doorway, he calls back. "If you try anything, I *will* kill him." Then, he shuts the door.

Opening the closet, I rattle hangers, talking aloud, knowing he's listening in. "Not that one, no, no, no, oh, yes! Gucci." I hear him chuckle and walk down the hall. Ditzy Eliana saves the day again. They really should stop underestimating me. I can be smart *and* well dressed.

"I'll be back with the wine, sweets," he yells.

I slip into the shirt, buttoning it up, knowing my nipples show through the fabric, and shake out my hair. I glance in the mirror as I lift his phone, powering it on and holding a pillow over it while singing to cover any sounds. I quickly dial Jaxx, knowing he will immediately answer a call from Richard.

LOVE REMEMBERS

CHAPTER EIGHTEEN

Andrew

"Have you located Douglass?" I shout, pacing in my office. How is it, no one knows anything? How is this man a fucking ghost? Not even I can cover my tracks so thoroughly.

"They have, boss. He's home with family. Police everywhere, though. Looks like some are headed our way," one of my men says from my doorway.

"What?! The police? Here? Why?" I step up to him.

"I don't know, boss. Just a tip that came in from your cop friend. Brown. Said to lock it all up. Now."

"Andrew! We have them!" Costin yells, running from the house with Jaxx.

"Lock it all down and get out! I don't give a fuck what happens here. I am getting my daughter back," I bellow, chasing after the boys.

Jaxx puts his phone on speaker, listening while he stares down at his phone.

"It's Richard. I can track him." Jaxx is barely audible.

"Richard? No..." When I hear what comes out of the phone, I nearly fall. I have been a fucking fool. I brought this man into her life. This is entirely my fault. I am a total failure, and I have allowed all of us to ruin my daughter. What have I done?

Eliana

"Tell me you've found her," he demands after one ring.

"Help us," I whisper but fumble the phone dropping it behind the table when I hear Richard approach the door. Rushing to the opposite end of the bed, I sit seductively, praying I can distract him long enough for the guys to get here. God let them hurry.

"Look at you." Richard approaches, licking his lips. "I have waited far too long for this. I am going to fucking wreck you."

He pushes me back onto the bed, pulling at the shirt and causing the buttons to scatter across the room. I squeeze my eyes closed tightly, seeing a pair of dark brown eyes lending me the strength I need to get through... to pretend I'm somewhere else, with someone else. Someone I love.

"That fucking Laporte boy had no idea what he had. I hate that he was inside you, but fucking Puckett just had to watch while the boy took your virginity. All the better I suppose." He shrugs. "I don't have the patience to be soft like he was, anyways."

"What?" I choke out, stunned and fighting to keep my emotions under control as my mind spins with this new information.

"He had to die, sweet girl. There was no other way." He squeezes my right breast while biting the other.

"Laporte? You mean Joshua? You didn't kill him, did you?" I sputter, the last question leaving me in a harsh whisper. It's not possible.... Is it?

"Yes, Joshua, and no, I didn't kill him per se." He smirks up at me like we're sharing an inside joke, and I want to vomit. "Only fools dirty their own hands in order to get what they need. Real men have the ability to make things happen *for* them, getting what they need *and* want. I want you. I *need* you. He was in my way. I refused to watch him with you for another second. You belong to me, always have. He had no right to touch you. I was always the puppet master, sweet girl. They killed the Laporte boy without hesitation simply because I pulled the right strings. See, Eliana? Now you get to have a *real* man. You're welcome." Richard grins down at me darkly. He's so detached, and the coldness I see in his eyes freezes my blood immediately, rendering what's left of my heart useless.

"Why? How?" I want to beg him to continue, but I'm unable to form a complete sentence. I am trembling from head to toe, shaken to my core. I knew he was evil, but he has gone to such lengths to destroy those I love. For what? This can't be all about an infatuation with me, could it? OMG, what about..."Puckett?"

"For us, obviously. Anything to get you here with me now. None of them were worthy anyways, not like I am. As for Puckett? He deserved everything he got. I made an exception for that pervert and killed him myself. Screamed like a bitch until I cut out his fucking tongue. Then, he just gurgled." He laughs, leaning down, kissing me hard, and suddenly forcing his index finger inside me. I gasp, unable to hide my reaction to the pain. "Relax, sweet girl. I'm going to make you feel good. Here, I'll turn on some music." He reaches for the table and his eyes narrow. Oh God, no. "Where the fuck is my phone?"

"What phone?" I sit up, attempting to distract him with a kiss, knowing that the guys won't be much longer. Someone has to be close by now. He's been talking forever. Bragging really.

Richard shoves me to the side and searches around the table, easily noticing the illuminated screen, then lifts the phone from the floor with a 'tsk.' Looking down at the cell, he quickly sits back down on the bed and grabs me by the hair, roughly pulling me into his lap. Hissing into my ear, he promises, "Big mistake, sweet girl. I'm going to enjoy killing Abel right in front of you." Then, he raises the phone to his head, speaking in a casual voice. "Jaxxson? How are you, dear boy? ...Such language... Yes, she's here... No, she's busy right now... Oh yeah? Such big threats for such a small man, Jaxxson... Tell me, son, how does it feel knowing that your incompetence made her such an easy target? That you will get to listen to her screams, helpless on the other side of the phone, knowing you could have stopped me, but instead your failure has guaranteed you will never get her back." He laughs, setting down the phone without ending the call. "Extra loud so he can hear you, sweet girl."

Biting my shoulder viciously, he forcefully shoves three fingers in me, laughing when I fail to hold in my scream at the dry intrusion and enjoying my attempts to wiggle out of his tight hold.

"Looks like our first time *will* be memorable," he says, tossing me onto the bed and quickly pulling off his pants as I crawl across the bed. As I reach the edge, he grabs my leg, yanking me back to him. When he positions himself to shove inside me, I pull back my leg and kick him flatfooted in the nose. Covering his face with both hands, he stumbles back and falls to the floor, shouting.

"You fucking cunt! Don't move!"

"Fuck that," I mumble, running from the room, grabbing a serrated knife from the kitchen, and burst into the living room. Hitting my knees in front of Abel, I gasp at how pale he is, but I cut the zip ties from his hands and ankles then tuck the knife into the front pocket of my ripped shirt. "Come on, big guy. Time to go. I need you to stand up for me. I'm not leaving you, and I can't carry you. You have to stand. Come on." I pull him to stand, but he sways, unable to put pressure on his injured leg.

"Don't fucking move, Eliana." I freeze, seeing the pistol aimed at Abel, center mass.

"Please, he didn't do anything. I'll stay with you. Please, just let him go." I beg, stepping forward, trying to position myself between Richard and Abel, knowing that he wants me too much to kill me.

"No, I'm sorry, not going to happen. I will not

cave this time, Eliana. You need to be taught a lesson, and this is the perfect time. You have practically begged for a firmer hand for years. I have been too easy on you since day one, showering you with gifts and affection. If I had been tougher on you before, none of this would have happened. I really thought that when I killed Joshua in front of you, it would be enough to break your stubborn streak, but it looks like you are going to need a lot more discipline. I am really going to enjoy putting you in your place, Eliana." He gives me a chilling grin, licking his lips.

"My mother killed Joshua, Richard. Why do you keep saying *you* killed him? What else have you done to us?" My voice wavers.

"Your whore of a mother-" He smiles darkly. "She hated your father with a passion that burned brighter than any love she could have ever had for you. I truly enjoyed showing her all the ways she could hurt him without him catching on. I helped her to toy with all of you. I used her hatred and desperation for vengeance to get me closer to this moment with you, all while keeping suspicions miles away from me. She was entertaining at times, but she tried to hurt *you,* so she had to die. It was rather nice being able to be the one to put that bullet in her back in the clearing. She talked too much. Riding over to rescue you with Andrew was one of my more impulsive decisions, but it was worth it. Speaking of your naïve father..." Richard sneers, raising the gun back up when we hear the nearing sounds of motorcycle engines. "Now, where were we?"

I step into Abel, giving him a quick shove, knowing he's already unsteady on his feet, and he falls right before Richard pulls the trigger. One. Two.

I hit my knees with a grunt and touch my stomach, confused when I feel something wet, "What?"

"No!" Abel bellows, covering my wound with his hands. "No, no, no."

Richard drops to my side, pulling me from an already weak Abel, and scooping me up in his arms, "Why? Why would you do that, Eliana? I love you. Why couldn't you just listen to me? Why does everything have to be a fight with you?"

"Because, Richard, Jamesons never submit," I

spit.

"You don't understand. I did this all for *you.* I love you. I know you love me, too. It didn't have to be like this. I could have made you happy."

"You could never have my heart, Richard. I gave it away years ago. The damn thing doesn't even reside in my own chest anymore. You need to understand this, Richard- I will *never* be yours. I would rather die, but-" I spit, pulling the knife from my shirt and jamming it into the same area they stabbed Joshua. "-I'm damn sure taking you with me." He drops me roughly to the hardwood floor with a stunned expression from the unexpected power shift.

I look him in the eyes, hissing, "You never loved me, Richard. I don't think you've ever loved anyone other than yourself. Not even your own daughter. What would she think of the man you've become? She loved you so much, worshiped the ground you walked on."

"What would she think?" He laughs painfully. "I'll have to ask her when I get to hell. That's if she can speak down there. I did cut out the bitch's tongue right before I killed her, just like Puckett. She just wouldn't keep her mouth closed. She knew what the consequences would be. Such a simple minded girl, a real disappointment."

"*You* killed her, too?"

"All for us. She was nothing compared to you." Richard lays back with a thud, chuckling. "They will all die out there you know? I have men positioned everywhere. I knew they would come. Unlike your father, I am *always* prepared. So listen closely, sweet girl. You are about to hear every single one of them die. I am all you have left, and you've buried a knife in my chest. Unappreciative brat. You will be alone forever because I can guarantee you none of them will make it in here to you." He turns his head to me, smiling as blood trickles from the corner of his mouth, and something in me breaks.

"Will you just fucking die already, you twisted bastard?!" I grab the hilt of the knife, pulling it from his chest with a sickening sound, gagging, and then bury it in his throat. One. Two times. "You are nothing! You lose, Richard. They *will* come for me. They always do. You. Lose."

The bikes shut off outside. Richard reaches for my hand, accepting his fate but unable to acknowledge my hatred for him in his final moments. Instinctively, I pull my hand back with a sneer. Keeping my gaze locked on his, I watch as the life fades from his eyes, and his blood pools around us, slowly merging with my own. Abel crawls to me, wrapping me in his arms, and tries to stem the flow of blood from my abdomen. We both jump at the sound of gunfire and shouting, knowing that our family is in trouble and that neither of us is physically capable of doing a fucking thing about it.

Attempting to stand, Abel collapses three times before giving up, wrapping me in his arms and rocking me again. "They're coming, Darlin'. Why didn't you just run when I told you to? Stay with me, E. Don't you leave me. You promised. You're fighting back, remember?"

"Tired of fighting, big guy. I love you. I love *all* of you. Tell them not to be sad. I'll be fine. Someone's already waiting on me." I wipe away his tears with shaky fingers, accidently smearing the blood covering my hands across his cheek, and turn when the door bursts open.

"Princess? No!" Costin bellows, running to me and scooping me up.

"There's my brave knight," I breathe out with a small smile, closing my eyes, truly grateful that my last minutes will be spent in his arms. "I missed him."

"No Princess, eyes open! If you go, I'll follow." He would, too, so I force my eyes open. "Abel, how bad?"

"Can't walk. It's my leg. I'll live, just get her out of here."

"I'll send someone back for you, man. Princess, hold on."

Bursting from the house, Costin runs, jumping from the porch, doing his best to shield me from the shots around us.

"Costin, is she-" Jaxx yells but jerks forward falling to the ground, not moving.

"No..." I whimper. "Help... him," I beg, fading.

"Run, Costin!" I hear Daddy shout as I lose the battle to stay conscious.

LOVE REMEMBERS

CHAPTER NINETEEN

Eliana

"Time to wake up," a warm breath fans across my face, smelling faintly of chocolate, reminding me of nights under the stars and-

"Charming?" My voice wavers.

"You were amazing, Angel. Open your eyes."

"No." I shake my head. "You won't be there. I can't. Not again."

"I'm here." He chuckles, and I feel his lips brush mine.

"Stay!" I pull him to me, deepening the kiss, my eyes popping open when his tongue brushes mine. "Charming-" I sob, "you're really here?

"More or less, Angel. Miss me?" His eyes are glassy as he brushes away my tears and pulls me onto his lap.

The porch swing sways under us, and I take in our surroundings. The sea air mixes with the faint smell of a charcoal grill while the sounds of children giggling and waves crashing to shore fill the air around me... the future we planned.

"Joshua, where are we?" I breathe, looking into his emerald eyes.

"After, Angel. This is where I wait." He smiles, brushing a stray hair from my cheek.

"I don't understand. Am I dead?"

"No, love, you're not dead, but I knew you needed to see me. We're still connected, Eliana. Feel." He places my hand on his chest as a tear trails down his beautiful cheek. "Even though my heart stopped beating in that life, it continues to beat *here* for you. I got to bring our love with me."

"I lost everything when you died."

"So build new with the love that didn't." He smiles.

"It's all my fault," I sob.

"No-" He's stern. "None of this was your fault, not even a little. Richard, Andrew, and your mother did this. Not you."

"The vent. I-"

"You freed me, love. You knew what was right, and you put me first, knowing it would hurt you. You are so brave, and I love you so very much." He runs a hand softly up and down my arm.

"I've betrayed you." I cry, clinging to his shirt. "I'm so angry and lost."

"No, Angel." He kisses my temple. "You've never betrayed me, not once. Let them take care of you. Let *him* love you. Let him in."

"Jaxx?" I ask.

"No, love." He shakes his head, "The knight who owns the other part of your heart. Let him save you again."

"I can't. Please, don't make me leave. I don't want to fight anymore. Just let me die. I want to stay here with you." I wrap my arms around him, holding tightly.

"You can't stay, Angel." He takes my face in his hands, tears rolling down both of our faces. "I need you to live for me. Don't waste a single second. Love, laugh, build that castle, and fill it with happiness. Shine, love. You are the light. You are *my* reason."

"No, Charming, not without you." I kiss him desperately, feeling myself fading from his after.

"I'm okay, Angel. We aren't finished, not forever. Love him in the life you have now, and I will wait for you in this one. It's okay to be in love with us both. I can see that now. It doesn't lessen what we have."

"Don't leave me," I beg.

"Never, ever." He smiles sadly, closing his eyes. When they open again, they twinkle. "The light, Angel you're haloed. So sad-" He kisses away my tears, losing the battle with his own again. "-but still so beautiful."

"I love you so much, Joshua," I sob.

"I love you, too." He places my hand on his chest, tapping twice. "It will always beat for you, through all of eternity and even after. You own my soul, Eliana. Be happy. Let *him* in. Love again. Promise me. No more waiting."

I nod reluctantly.

"That's my girl." He smiles.

Holding him close, I bury my face in his neck, breathing him in. Knowing what he's about to say and not wanting to hear it.

"I need you to wake up now, Angel." He kisses me softly, not wanting to let go any more than I do but knowing we don't have a choice.

"Just a little longer?" I beg, brokenly. "Tell me a story, Charming. The happy one."

"Okay, Angel, once more." He wraps me tightly in his arms and pushes the swing into a calming rock. "Once upon a time there was a beautiful Princess. She was strong and brave. Loved by many, but blessed only two with her love in return. Those men knew the value of the gift bestowed upon them and treasured it always..."

LOVE REMEMBERS

CHAPTER TWENTY

Costin

"Please, wakeup, Princess. Please come back. You're safe now. It's okay," I plead. She has been out of surgery for six hours and still hasn't opened her eyes.

"Let her rest, Costin. The doctors said she will be fine. She just needs to sleep." Jaxx eases into the chair across from me but leans forward, cringing.

The vest saved his life, but the cracked ribs still fucked him up. "She's crying, Cos. Why is she crying?"

"That's what I mean." I kiss the tear from her cheek. "I should get the doctor. She might be in pain."

"Thanks for getting the door, prick." Abel wheels into the room as I'm standing. "I mean, did you really need to leave me to get here faster? I could understand if- Why is she crying?"

"Don't leave," she mumbles brokenly, still sleeping. "Tell...story...happy one."

"Did someone bring her bag?" Jaxx looks around frantically.

"Right here." Jonah strolls in, carrying her old Sleeping Beauty book bag over his shoulder.

"Manly." Abel snorts.

"I found the book, but it's falling apart. Want me to go buy her a new one?" Jonah offers.

"Never," she whispers roughly, pulling all of our attention to her.

We all go to speak at once, but she shakes her head. "Not right now guys. I can't." Tears roll down her cheeks, and my heart breaks.

"Are you in pain, little wave?" Jonah walks up, standing beside me. He gently moves a lock of hair from her face, causing her to smile sadly up at him.

What? I'm gonna stab him. I curl my lip until I hear her soft laughter.

"A little, but I'll be okay. A wave, huh?"

"You fought back pretty fucking hard, beautiful." He leans over, kissing her head, causing both Jaxx and me to growl.

"Good to see you up, Darlin'. I'm going to head down to the waiting room to let everyone know you're awake. Jonah, why don't you come with me before you end up injured, too?" Abel chuckles.

"Abel? Thank you." Eliana sniffs.

"For what, Darlin'?" He wheels in closer, taking her hand.

"For fighting for me. Your leg, he said-" She hiccups a small sob, and Abel's chin trembles.

"No, Darlin', thank *you*. I remember what happened in that house." We all turn to him questioningly, but he shakes his head. "It's not my story to share. I remember though. What you did, sacrificed, to keep me alive. *You* did the real fighting. You're not a little wave. You're a fucking tsunami. I love you, Darlin', and I am so proud of you. Now rest." He wipes tears from his face, and I am sick with the thought of what put them there.

"I *knew* you were listening to us that night." Jonah shakes his head, placing a hand on Abel's shoulder and giving it a squeeze before pushing Abel's chair from the room.

"We'll come back by later, beautiful."

"Okay," she whispers, looking down and twisting her hands in her lap when they close the door behind them.

"What happened?" all three of us ask together.

"Princess, did he-" I swallow hard.

Eliana

I take a deep breath. "What did the doctors say?"

"They said there was... trauma but wouldn't say anymore." Jaxx takes my hand. "Baby, he didn't? Did he?"

I should lie, tell them he never had the chance to touch me, but I can't. I promised Joshua I would try to be happy, and I can't do that if we continue this dance.

"Not exactly," I force out.

"What does that mean, Eliana?" Jaxx jumps to his feet, taking my face in his hands gently and searching my eyes.

"Princess?" Costin is tugging at his hair beside me.

"I don't want to talk about it, guys. You trained me to survive, and I did. I fucking killed him," I cry. "I did kill him, right?!"

"He's fucking dead," Jaxx confirms. "Wait, *you* did that?"

I nod. "It was him or Abel. I would do it again."

They sit on either side of my bed.

"Your screams?" Jaxx asks, and I nod again.

"He touched me, but that's all I'm saying. I will not let this define me or paint any more pictures in your heads. He has no hold here. Not anymore." I wipe my eyes with the back of my hand. "He had Joshua killed."

"We know, baby. We put it together before but didn't have a name. When your call came in, we realized how blind we had been."

"Where's Daddy? I heard him there."

"He ran, Princess. He stepped up when it mattered though. He loves you in his own way. He wanted to be here. It's just that Richard had a ton of dirt on him that he turned over right before taking you, including the house fire from the night we found you, the murder of his brother and father, and the details of him manipulating you to take control of your inheritance. Turns out, you don't have to marry at all. He just wanted a man beside you, willing to do anything to keep you sheltered. That way, he could get your husband to sign over control of your grandfather's fortune to him. He knew Joshua would. Turns out both he and Jaxx had already agreed to it so long as you were provided for and safe," Costin huffs.

"Coming after me in the end doesn't fix everything he's done," I spit. "That's why he wouldn't let you be with me? Because you are too unpredictable and would have probably just told him to fuck off?"

"We all know how that would have gone," Jaxx snarls.

"Come here, Jaxxson." I open my arms, and he gently lays his head on my chest.

"I'm sorry, baby." He turns, burying his face against my gown, soaking it with his tears. "I keep failing you."

"Listen to me, Jaxx. None of what he said to you on that phone was true." I run my fingers through his hair soothingly, the way he always does for me. "You did everything you could to protect me, and you succeeded. When the time came for me to fight back, I could. Because. Of. You. Teaching me how to defend myself may have been a group effort, but *you* taught me how to be smart about it. I only made it out of there because you taught me how to stay calm and think. You gave me the strength I needed to get through it, and I did. So, no more guilt. I love you so much, and you will always be my person. You have to know when to accept that sometimes things happen beyond our control, no matter how hard we try to prevent them. We didn't do this; they did. We were simply trying to survive, and we *did*."

"When did you get so wise?" He smiles through his tears.

"Someone I love dearly sat me down and talked to me." I smile back.

"When?" Jaxx raises a brow.

"After," I breathe out softly.

"You're still an oddity, Munchkin."

"Munchkin?"

"We both know where your heart lies, and you're no longer bound to me." He shrugs sadly, looking over at Costin, who is standing, facing the window.

"I don't regret a single second of us, Jaxx."

"No?"

"Never-ever, Jaxxson. I love you so very much. Thank you for always putting me first. I don't always deserve you, but I am so grateful that you chose to stay with me through it all anyways."

"I love you, too, Munchkin." He leans over and kisses me softly. "Talk to him. You're free now. It's time to listen to your heart. It does matter. I'm going to go speak with the police. I'll be back." He slips quietly from the room, and I look at Costin.

"Costin-"

"Princess-"

We laugh, speaking at the same time.

"I'm still in love with you, brave knight," I blurt out through my tears, and he spins, practically running to my bedside and dropping to his knees.

"You love me, Princess?" He takes my hand,

trembling.

"I do. So very much," I reply softly, barely holding it together.

"And what about Joshua? Will you *be* with me?" he begs, hope filling his eyes.

"He still owns part of my heart, Cos. He always will. But now, I know that it's all right to feel that way. That I can love you both, and it doesn't diminish what I feel for either of you. It never has." I smile softly through my tears, scooting carefully to the left, needing him to come closer.

"I know, Princess." He quickly climbs in next to me, holding on as if he is afraid I may disappear any second.

"I'm done waiting for my happily ever after, brave knight. I am ready to be happy again... with you. That is if you still want me?" My voice shakes. I know that I am no longer the girl he fell for, and he may have changed his mind. I am unsure of who I am anymore. My soul is damaged. My heart has been shattered. My trust in everything was broken. My entire universe is in ruins. But at the bottom of it all, there is hope... hope that I can heal, that I am more than the sum of my tragedies, and that maybe

Costin was wrong about the Princess and her Knight all along. Maybe they *can* have their happily ever after.

"I will *always* want you." Costin leans his forehead against mine, smiling gently through his own tears.

"Always, brave knight?" I whisper, needing to hear him say it more than I need my next breath.

"Always, Princess." Always... I'm his.

"This is it, it's us. This is our shot. What will you do with it, Costin?"

"I'm pretty sure it all starts with true love's kiss, Princess." He grins, carefully pulling me closer until our chests touch and cradling my face in his palms.

"Then kiss me, Costin, and never let go again." I exhale breathlessly, knowing what's coming next.

"I thought you would never fucking ask," he rushes out, lips crashing into mine. This kiss isn't stolen in a dark corner or empty closet. We are free, and this love is ours to keep. He deepens our kiss, claiming me. His love pushes away every shadow, every sadness, and every pain. They aren't gone forever. I know that, but right now, things are pure light. Thank you, Charming. I will never stop loving you, but thank you for showing me that it's okay to love him, too.

"You brought back the light, Costin," I whisper in total awe of this moment with him.

"Our love brought back the light, Princess." He leans in, placing a gentle kiss on my neck, inhaling deeply. When he lifts his head from my shoulder with a small smile, I can see everything shining back through his tear-filled eyes. Every emotion I was sure I, alone, felt. All of our past. Our love, loss, struggle, pain, laughter, tears, and now... there is more. A future. A promise. Now we can have more, together. Because there, in his loving gaze, is something I should have seen from the beginning. The truth. I was never alone. The Knight didn't really abandon his Princess. He sacrificed himself just as he predicted he would. I'm his...

"Always." We say together right before our lips meet again. This is where I will rebuild. This love will survive. This man is my future.

CHAPTER TWENTY-ONE

Andrew

The Laporte house has gone silent. I know Douglass was the one responsible for leaking my information to the authorities. He knew about my daughter, hurt those kids, and used his son's love for Eliana to get close to me. He played both sides, finally settling on the losing end. He knows I am coming for him. He is the reason I can't be with my daughter. Not that she wants me there. I can give her this, though. I will free them and make sure Douglass suffers for what he has done. Eliana ended Richard. She is stronger than I ever imagined, and she is a fucking vision. I know they could handle him, but what can I say... I have always enjoyed the screams.

I creep into the house silently and head down the hall where I hear harsh whispers.

"Put down the knife, Dame. It's okay now. It's over. I'm okay. See?" A clatter that I assume is the knife falling echoes through the room, and I slowly open the door, looking in. The man wraps her in his arms, both covered in red, and Douglass Laporte lays motionless at their feet in a pool of his own blood. Well, I'll be damned.

"It's okay. You're my girl, Lilabelle Fayre Maxfield. I am so sorry. You and me. Forever. I love you, Dame." He rocks side to side with her in his arms, humming softly. Costin was right; they are enchanting. Covered in blood, the pull is even stronger.

"There you are." Kendrick smiles down, kissing her gently when she finally stops shaking. "We need to go, Dame. We can't stay here."

"No, you can't." I step into the room.

"Get back!" Kendrick yells, grabbing the knife from the floor and stepping in front of her.

"I won't hurt you. I came here to..." I gesture to Douglass.

"Oh yeah? Why do you suddenly care now?" he spits.

"My daughter. Eliana. You know her, don't you?" They both nod solemnly.

"Is she okay?" A soft voice floats from behind the man, and though he attempts to move her back, she ducks under his arm, still peeking at me.

"She is. Are you?" I ask, the vulnerability in her gaze reminding me so much of my Poppet's the night I found her that I want to take her and shield her the way I failed to do with Poppet. But it's too late for both of them. The damage is done.

"I am. That box is for her. They are Joshua's treasured memories. He showed me a picture of her from it once, and I knew he would want her to have them. Nothing good should be left in this place," she replies firmly, tipping her chin up and stepping around Kendrick to pick up the small box from the floor. He grabs her arm when she steps towards me.

"Lilabelle, no."

"Listen to him, little dancer. You need to leave here. Trust no one, especially not me. And I can't take that." I nod to the box. "The police." I chuckle, thinking about the man hunt… if I didn't have the friends that I have, I would be fucked. It pays to know people… well, it pays to know shit *about people.*

"Tell you what. I will handle this mess, make sure none of this is traced back to you, and you can take that to my daughter?"

"You said not to trust you," Kendrick snaps.

"I did, but this is mutually beneficial. I have the connections you need to make this disappear, and you have the access I have been denied."

"Okay," Lilabelle whispers, taking Kendrick's hand.

"Clean up first. You can't go anywhere looking like that. You have thirty minutes before the crew will be here, so make it quick." I gesture to the bathroom, and they turn to leave together. "Wait. Abel. He's your father."

"I know that," she says coldly from the doorway.

"You can trust him. He's a good man."

"*That.* I don't know. He never even tried." She shakes her head.

"He wants you."

"We'll see..." she says, turning again to leave.

Kendrick looks to me when she walks into the bathroom, out of earshot.

"Abel?"

"You can trust him. If there ever comes a time... Jaxx, Costin, my daughter. Those four will help you. Don't figure you will have much of a choice in the end. I never did. Eliana is relentless, and those boys would follow her anywhere. So they will find you eventually. Actually, finding people is Jaxx's specialty. Besides, you can't just hide forever. How will you live? Money?"

"Well, Andrew. We know how to stay hidden and quiet... it's our specialty. She is my only concern. I will make sure she is safe and has what she needs. There is nothing I won't sacrifice. Nothing I won't do for her." He steps from the room, calling back, "If he wants his daughter back, he will have to prove it... not just to her but to me as well. And Andrew, that's not going to be an easy sale."

I nod to him, understanding. "I have the same

path ahead of me. I understand. Good luck. Keep her safe. Trust or not. If you keep her from him and something else happens, you are a dead man."

Shaking his head with a humorless laugh, he answers, "If something happens to her, I can guarantee you that I am already dead. You have no idea the life we have led and the sacrifices I have made. She is as much mine as I am hers. There is no life without her."

"Good man."

"Andrew, thanks for handling this sack of shit, and good luck." He walks into the bathroom with her, closing the door behind him.

Costin

"Oh! I'm so sorry." We glance to the door at the sound of a soft feminine voice. Lilabelle. "I just wanted to drop this box off. Andrew said-"

"Come on, Dame. We should go." Kendrick pulls her behind him and places a warn shoebox on the floor, scooting it to us with his foot while staring at me with distrust.

"Wait!" I step forward.

"I don't think so, man. This was a mistake," he says, inching her closer to the exit, but she doesn't budge. "Run, Dame."

"Who are you?" Eliana eases herself up slowly on the bed.

"Princess-" I need to keep them here, but I didn't have a chance to explain all of it. I know this is going to upset her.

"No. I know you. Both of you. Please, stay. We won't hurt her," E begs.

"And him? I've seen him before," Kendrick sneers, jerking his chin in my direction.

"You have?" Eliana looks up at me.

"The basement, Princess. Douglass brought them. I never touched her." I look from my girl to Kendrick. "I won't hurt her, either. We have been searching for you both. Abel is desperate-"

"Abel?" E asks, confused.

"My father. Desperate for what?" Lilabelle's sweet voice turns icy at the mention of her father.

"He wants you home, safe. With him," I plead.

"Now? I don't need him *now*. My mother told me he would come for me every day until they killed her. She said he was a good man. He would save us. He *never* came. But *they* did."

"Oh, God, no." Eliana breathes out, wiping away a tear, and Lilabelle nods once.

"He didn't know-" I try to defend.

"Liar! My mother died trying to keep us safe. Where was he then? Where was he when she gave her life, trying to keep *them* away? To keep us safe where there were only monsters and darkness! How dare you say those things! She would never have told me that he would come if he didn't know. My father let them have us! He never cared!" Her tiny body begins to shake all over, and she lets out the saddest whimpers I have ever heard. More wounded than even my Princess'. What hell have these two survived?

Kendrick pulls her to his chest, rocking her to a tune he softly hums, and seemingly erases everything outside of their tiny bubble. "It's okay. You're my girl, Lilabelle Fayre Maxfield. I am so sorry. You and me. Forever. I love you, Dame." She looks up at him, and he kisses the tears from her cheeks. "There she is."

"You're them, aren't you? You were with me in

that basement, but they took you away." E sobs, and I wrap myself around her.

"For pictures." Kendrick nods solemnly. "They sold us quickly after you were taken, though."

"Sold you?! Where?" E presses the remote, raising the head of the bed until she cringes.

"Careful, Princess," I whisper, lowering it slightly, removing the pressure that sitting creates on her incision.

"Douglass Laporte," I answer, and Lilabelle shudders in Kendrick's arms.

"Douglass Laporte?! I- wha- Costin, you knew about this?" Eliana rears back, clearly distraught.

"Not until a couple weeks ago, but we didn't know *who* they were. We were trying to find out, though. When we found the photos in Joshua's room, we thought we had everything figured out, but it was bigger..." I try to explain, hanging my head. "I'm sorry, Princess."

"I trust you, Cos. You said Joshua? He would never-" Eliana shakes her head back and forth quickly.

"He didn't. Joshua tried to help us," Lilabelle whispers. "He told us all about you. That we could survive this, too. When he didn't come back-" She sobs and walks right into my Princess' open arms with Kendrick close on her heels, still watching me.

"He loved you so much. He was nothing like his father. He was the only man I ever trusted with my Dame. He was a good guy." Kendrick lowers his head, running a hand over her hair.

"Where is Douglass?" I ask, and Lilabelle suddenly pulls away, tucking back into Kendrick's side, and wraps her arms tightly around his waist.

"Gone," He grunts, running a hand up and down her back.

"Gone?" I raise a brow. They couldn't have... could they?

"Forever. Tell your father thank you, Eliana. I know he was a bad man, but- there are worse. He cares-" She spins to the door with wide eyes when we hear Abel and Jaxx getting close to the room.

"We need to move. Come on, Dame."

"Wait. Please. Abel's not a bad guy. Just give him a chance to explain. I know it seems scary, but he's not one of *them*. He's kind, gentle, protective... I couldn't have made it without him," E pleads.

"Thing is, Eliana, we *did* make it without him. We

didn't have a choice," Lilabelle sneers.

"Don't go. E's right. He really wants to help you."
I step forward, and Kendrick slides between us.

"If he wants me, tell him... tell him to actually
look this time." Lilabelle nods to the box, and I hand
it to E hesitantly. "That's all for you. I tucked in an
extra file for you. It explains the false information
your dad was given on Joshua. He wasn't cheating
on you. He was with us. Helping us. Photos only tell
a partial truth, and things aren't always as they
seem. Some are hard to look at, but...I'm tired of
hiding. The rest-" She brightens a little and offers
Eliana a kind smile. "- the rest is *you*. He told me
once that the box contained pieces of all the best
moments in his life." She looks into Eliana's eyes,
choking back a small sob. "You were his reason."
Eliana gasps, hugging the box tightly to her chest,
"Keep his-"

The door opens, and Abel freezes, taking in his
daughter close up for the first time. "Lilabelle,
honey-" Abel pleads softly, reaching for her hand,
but she stumbles back into Kendrick with a
whimper.

"Kendrick," she wheezes, gripping his shirt.

"I gotcha, Dame." He immediately sweeps her up and runs from the room with her in his arms.

"Wait! Please!" Abel shouts, trying to maneuver his chair back out to chase her. "Someone stop them!"

"No, Abel," E shouts, trying to sit up and crying out in pain, pulling our attention back to her.

"Princess." I panic, rushing back to her side, and Jaxx bursts through the door. Of course, he heard her.

"Munchkin, are you okay? Was that who I thought it was?" Jaxx looks around frantically. "Should I call down?"

"I'm fine. I'm fine. Just listen!" Eliana shouts. "All of you. She's not ready. She has been through hell, and she is finally free. Give them a chance to fly. If you want to know her, let her find herself, and then *prove it.* It's not your fault, and it's not fair, but this isn't about you. Yeah? Let her heal." She motions for Abel, and Jaxx helps straighten the chair, pushing it to her bed.

"How bad is she, Darlin'? Can I fix what they did to her?" Abel crumbles, putting his head in both hands, crying.

"It's not good." She lifts her hand, placing it against his cheek and wiping away a tear with her thumb. "But she is a wave, too, Abel. I saw it in her eyes, and she's not alone. He loves her so much you can feel it."

I lift a small notecard taped to the top of the box she left, addressed to E, and smile, reading the short message.

"Read this, Abel." She hands the card to him with a smirk. "Seems I was wrong about her being a wave after all. Turns out she's a damn storm, and she will need your help before she's done."

'One down. Three to go. If my father really wants to help me like Andrew claims he does, then tell him to come find us.

It's time we fight back,

Loreley and Azrail'

"The names?" Abel questions.

"They have taken back their lives. They are no longer victims, Abel; they are the bringers of death. You want your daughter? Find her and help her end this." She presses a button reclining the head of her bed with a small sleepy smile.

"We've beaten worse, Abel. You aren't alone in

this. We *will* find her," Jaxx promises, striding up and placing a hand on Abel's shoulder.

"Together," Eliana whispers.

"Together," we promise.

"Always." I smile at her.

My beautiful strong Princess. Through it all, she is still pure light. I may have hated Joshua for having her when I couldn't, but he was right about one thing. She was worth the wait.

LOVE REMEMBERS

CHAPTER TWENTY-TWO

Eliana

I take in the dark room, listening carefully to make sure my guys are all asleep, and then place a hand on the box still resting on my lap. I can't put it down, but can I open it? Should I? I just let Costin back in. Would it hurt him?

"You can look, Princess. It's okay." I jump when Costin speaks.

"Shit! You scared me, Cos. You could have told me you were still awake," I hiss, pressing my hands to my chest.

"Oh… yeah… I'm still awake, E." He chuckles, standing and walking over to the bed. "Scoot over. My ass is numb from that chair."

"Super creepy to watch people sleep, Cos." I laugh as he carefully helps me move over a bit, making room for him."

"Huh…" He shrugs. "I thought girls found it romantic."

"Maybe if you were gazing lovingly while lying beside her, but *you* were sitting like a pervy bushwhacker in a dark corner." I do my best to keep a straight face.

"A bushwhacker?" He chuckles.

"You heard me, creepo. Doodling your Baby Fetcher while watching me sleep… you should be ashamed."

"Doodling my Baby Fetcher?!" He laughs.

"No? How about Sex Pistol? Pleasure Pump? Excalibur? Lap Rocket? Oh! Your Love Dart!" I nod quickly. "That one's gonna stick!"

"It's far too manly to be called a love dart." Costin

laughs, sticking out his tongue and scrunching his face.

"Too late, what's done is done." I laugh enjoying the lightness of the moment.

Sighing, I shift slightly, leaning my head on his shoulder, but tip the small box over on its side, and sober, noticing some of its contents have spilled out.

"Cos-" My voice wavers. "I love you, but his absence... it still hurts. Why did this happen to us?" My tears spill over, and I look into his eyes, begging for answers I know he doesn't have.

"I don't know, Princess. It's not fair, and I wish I could fix it. I've tried. But we can't change what happened. All we can do is move forward and make the most of what we have now." My heart sinks with the thought of leaving Joshua behind, but Costin surprises me when he slowly leans forward, pulling my necklace from my shirt, and tenderly places the ring, urn, and locket against my chest. "You can take his love with us, Princess. He once promised me that he would love you enough for us both, and he kept that promise. Now, I'll do the same for him. I'm going to give you the future you wanted, and if you let me, I'll help you remember him. Just don't hide from me, okay?" He brushes his thumb gently across my lip. "I love you."

"There's my brave knight," I whisper. This is the Costin I fell in love with. He'll let me hide when I need to but never alone. "I love you, too. Always have."

I lift the envelope addressed to me in the same script as the note to Abel and place it on the table beside my hospital bed.

"Jaxx can have that. I don't need to see what's inside." And I mean it.

"You don't want to check?" Costin raises a brow.

"No, I trust him, Cos. He wasn't *that* man. I have always known that. Why do you think I let it go so easily when he came back? I know his heart just like I know yours. I don't need any proof beyond that, and I have already seen enough bad. Jaxx can decide if any of it will be useful in helping Abel find Lilabelle and Kendrick, and then we can destroy all of it when they are home with us. I don't want any of those images left, and I want our family whole." Costin nods.

"I think that's a good idea." He leans forward,

placing a kiss on my nose, then looks down at the items still in my lap. "And the rest?"

"I can't let him fade away, Cos. He deserves more." I brush away a few tears.

"I agree, Princess." He nods, picking up a photo from the pile with a grin. "I remember this one. Wrecking ball Eliana decided she was going to mow the lawn."

"Oh, lord." I groan, looking down at the image of me at nearly twelve years old, wearing Abel's boots, Jaxx's new motorcycle helmet, and my overalls, pushing an old lawnmower I found in the garage.

"Pretty sure *you* were the only thing that survived this little mishap without a scratch. I thought Jaxx was going to have a coronary when it rolled into the pool." He laughs.

"Not my fault. Faulty machinery. I asked Joshua. He agreed." I shrug.

"One hundred percent your fault. He just enjoyed watching us clean up your chaos. Then, the gas floated out of the tank and to the top of the pool!" He doubles over laughing. "Andrew had to call in a special crew to clean it. When he asked, all you said was, 'It was for science, Daddy. Are you trying to stifle my pursuit of knowledge?' And he laughed. The shit you got away with is mind boggling."

"Well, taught ya stuff, didn't I?" I jab him in the side.

"Like?"

"Like…" I tap my chin. "Gasoline floats; lawnmowers don't. That's a two-fer. You're welcome. Um, don't jump out of windows unless you want to break your arm. Cows are for cuddles. Whores give you chlamydia which makes your love wand shrivel up and fall off. You took care of that, right?" I laugh at his deadpan expression and continue. "I am an ocean of creatively earned knowledge, Cos. Show respect for the process."

"Uh-huh. I'll be sure to remember that. Thanks for the life lessons, Eliana."

"A debt you shall repay in cupcakes, brave knight," I tut then pick up another photo. "Thanksgiving."

"Ugh. That's the year you told everyone you were vegetarian and could only eat desserts, isn't it? How many pies did you have before you puked?" He shakes his head.

"I had four, and I stand by my decision. Even with

the puking, I don't regret it. Best holiday ever." I shrug, shuffling through the stack, suddenly speechless. "I can't believe he kept all of these."

"I can. These are the things that matter the most, E," he says, placing some folded up notes and cards atop the others I am separating from the photos. "I kept all of mine, too."

"You did?"

"Yeah." He offers me a half smile, "Everything you ever drew, wrote, colored, and made... everything you gave me from the day we met. I have it all. Right down to the handmade wrapping paper."

"I didn't know. I thought-"

"I get it, Princess. I didn't expect you to do the same after everything that happened." He runs a hand through his hair, shifting on the mattress. "I just... I don't know... I wanted you to-"

"I did, too, Cos. Through everything, I loved you both. Separate but together. Even when you... yeah. I still kept it all. You were always part of me even when you weren't."

"Yeah?" He takes my hand, giving it a gentle squeeze.

"Of course." I smile softly, lifting up the next photo from Joshua's collection. "For a couple of broken kids, we formed an awesome little family, Cos." I show him the image of our group standing by the pool in our swimsuits, me sandwiched between him and Joshua. "As bad as things got, we still had some great times."

Draping an arm around my shoulders, he pulls me closer to rest my head on his shoulder. "We got lucky."

"Most of the rest of the time, we fought for it." I sigh. "You think it will ever get easier? We aren't finished fighting. Abel needs us."

"I know." He kisses my head. "But we'll get through it. Let's just enjoy the peace we have right now and leave the worry for tomorrow. Okay?"

"I like that plan, Cos. Remember this?" I ask, holding up another.

Photo after photo, year after year, and memory after memory, we spend the night in laughter and tears, remembering Joshua, keeping our past alive, and allowing the rest of the world to fade away. Together.

Tomorrow, we can worry, but tonight, nothing

exists outside of this hospital room where the love between a fallen knight and his broken princess is finally worthy of a happy ending.

EPILOGUE

I smile at my reflection, turning from side to side, watching my dress swoosh around my feet. I breathe deeply, taking a moment to appreciate the silence before Jaxx comes to collect me.

Reaching for my shoes, I gasp when I see the Fendi box where my Manolo Blaniks should be. I rip off the lid, muffling a sob when I see the glitter covered pink heels and note inside. Taking a deep breath, I peel open the envelope and wipe away a tear as I begin to read.

'Poppet,

I'm not a good man. I'm not even an okay man. Truth be told, I'm a monster. I have done horrible things. My soul is tainted, and my whole life, I wanted nothing but revenge. That is until you. The day we found you in that basement, my life changed. I fought it, pushing myself to do horrible things. I tried not to fall for your sweet little smile, but I failed. The problem is it's not the only thing I failed at. I failed to keep you safe. I failed to put you first. I failed as a father. The men I employed did what I refused to do every day. Maybe that made me feel better about my actions. Maybe it was an excuse. Either way, it was wrong. Know this, Poppet. I do love you. My black heart is capable of love- imagine that. I want to be there, walking you down the aisle, but I know I don't deserve that honor. I'm not better. I haven't turned my life around. I am still the monster I was before. Only difference is that I am actually thinking of you first this time. I love you, Poppet, and I hope these shoes help you to believe that. I know how much you loved your first pair when you were nothing more than a tiny doll asking me to brush her hair. I will be watching. Be happy, Poppet. Go sparkle.

Love Remembers,

Daddy

"Oh Daddy," I sob, clutching the letter to my chest.

"Ready, Munchkin? Costin is getting antsy; not sure he's going to wait much longer for his bride." Jaxx walks in. "Are you okay? What is it?"

I hand him the letter.

"He does love me." I smile through my tears.

"He does. You forgive him?"

"Not yet, Jaxx, but this tells me that one day I might be able to." I lean over, sliding my feet into the heels, and turn to the mirror, touching up my makeup.

"You look stunning, Munchkin." Jaxx spins me into his chest, laughing, but goes silent when my body connects with his, and I place a hand on his chest.

"Jaxx?"

"I love you so much, Munchkin." He smiles sadly

then steps back. "Let's get you to your fiancée, shall we?"

"Wait, Jaxx. I'm sorry."

"No, Munchkin. Please, don't be sorry. I don't regret one second of my time with you." He repeats my words to him, and I lean in, kissing his cheek.

"Me neither, Jaxx. You'll always be my person."

"Yeah?"

"Yeah." I hug him. "Forever and ever."

"Come on you two. Time's a wasting." Abel pushes into the room, leaning slightly on a cane. He's healing more every day, but not nearly fast enough for his liking. He is ready to find his daughter, and I don't blame him. Thankfully, Jaxx needed something to occupy his time. It won't be long now.

"Coming, big guy. You two ready?" I take each of their arms, walking from the room and to the beginning of the aisle. "Oh my," I sob out, spotting Costin in his tux, staring back at me.

"First step, Darlin'. Let's start your happy ever after. What do ya say?"

"Yesss!" I breathe out and place my glittery Fendi heel onto the pink carpet, taking my first step toward my Knight.

Costin

She comes into view, and everything stops. I can't breathe. I can't think. I can't... wait. Fuck this. I storm down the aisle, meeting her halfway, and kiss her. "Mine."

"Costin?" She gasps, looking up at me, smiling.

"You said no more waiting." I lean over, sweeping her up into my arms, and carry her to the altar.

"Put me down." She giggles.

"Never." I laugh, kissing her forehead, cheek, nose, and finally her lips.

"Oh, so you're just gonna hold me?"

"Always." I smile at her.

"Always." She nods. "I really like the sound of that."

"Me too, Princess. Me too."

The End... for now.

UPCOMING RELEASES

Andrew- Twisted Redemption

Jaxx- Severed Bonds

Jonah- Tangled Melody

Abel- Crippled Devotion

ALSO FROM WINTER PAIGE

Devastation Duet:

Shattered Lies (Book 1)

Broken Trust (Book 2)

STALK ME:

Facebook: WinterPaigeWrites

Readers Group: Winter Paige's Readers

Email: WinterPaigeWrites@gmail.com

Amazon: amazon.com/author/winterpaige

Goodreads: winterpaigewrites

Instagram: winterpaigewrites/

ACKNOWLEDGEMENTS

What a ride. Two books from first word to paperback in two months is crazy insane, and honestly, I still haven't processed it. I am going to give this another go... I know I will forget someone, sorry.

Diksha, AGAIN, you are my freaking rock, girl. You corral my ducks into a zigzag, attempt to keep me on schedule, and deal with my constant torment. YOU keep me going. Thank you for being you *and* me. Thank you for posting, researching, organizing, and trying your best to make me adult (I mean you failed at that, but you tried super hard). If it wasn't for you, these books wouldn't have gone any further than the scribbles on a shoebox. You pushed me and didn't stand down when I pushed back. Thank you for being awesome Mrs. Costin Andrews... btw, I am telling him about Jonah. I love you, Bitch.

Jocqueline, you are an inspiration and, in all

honestly, my hero. Thank you for your faith in me, your support, and for not strangling me for being the hyperactive squirrel that I am. Thank you for taking a chance on me and giving me back my confidence. You helped me believe in myself again.

Dawn, I can't comma to save my life. You have taken pages of chaos and turned them into actual English, like whoa. Thank you for helping out a confused newbie. Thank you for putting up with my intentional use of phrases that make you cringe knowing I only do it for my own amusement. Thank you for correcting the grunts and moans – haha. Thank you for being the kickass English wizard that you are because, let's face it, I'm garbage without you.

Trenda. You took a scuffed up rock and polished it into a gem. Without you, I would still be an unrefined mess of time jumps and skips. You turned me into what I am. Thank you for being patient, for focusing my ADHD, and seeing potential under the mess. I love you, lady!

To my family, I am a mess. I am a garbage human. I am 90% caffeine and sugar and 10% human-ish. Thank you for not complaining too much or calling

CPS over the frozen foods and general filth... I love you all.

My inner circle: Katie, Nichole, Shonda, Morgen, Diksha, and Jayce... my Devastating Ladies! You all keep me going. Your tears feel my soul, and your yelly messages keep me writing. I love every one of you!

Morgen, the sender of all things good and wonderful... I'm out of candy... and Mamoa. Send halp!

Melissa Teo, LOOK AT MY COVERS!!! Just look at them, they are gorgeous! My gosh woman, you are a f'ing rock star! Thank you for always being there, for being brutally honest, and fixing what was broken. I love your face!

Alyssa, thank you for being my friend. For listening to my rambling and putting up with my crazy writing mood swings. Thank you for getting so dang excited when I published the first time. I'm not famous, but you made me feel like it. You are the brightest star, and I can't wait to see where life takes you!

Amber and Krys, thank you for helping out clueless friend. Anyone who can do what you two have done when the only directions I send are 'I don't know. I am garbage. Do what you do 'cause it's hella awesome," deserves a medal.

To my readers: I cannot believe you are actual people... how is this real life? Thank you from the bottom of my twisted heart. I will continue writing as long as you all continue reading!

Love Remembers,
Always.
Winter Paige

ABOUT THE AUTHOR

Winter Paige is a budding author in the genre of dark romance. Born in the Capital city of WV she enjoys reading, traveling, and producing audio books. Winter lives with her husband, four children and a cat she despises ... and is tormented daily by chickens.

Made in the USA
Middletown, DE
31 October 2020

23060807R00156